The Choice

Luke Seibert

Luke Seibert

Copyright © 2018 Luke Seibert

All rights reserved.

Cover design courtesy of Levi Seibert and Stephen Wess.

All Scripture quotations are taken from the King James Version. Public Domain.

ISBN: 1725565994
ISBN-13: 9781725565999

DEDICATION

I would like to dedicate this book to Charles Hardy, who has been my carpentry instructor, my mentor, and my friend. In many ways, he has been to me what Samuel Kouffers is to Peter Brenton in this book. Thank you, Mr. Hardy, for everything you have taught me both in and out of the cabinet shop, and especially for always exhorting me to follow the Lord Jesus Christ in every area of life.

ACKNOWLEDGMENTS

I would like to thank my father, Darren Seibert, for his constant encouragement and positive feedback as I have written and published this book. I would also like to thank my mother, Carrie Seibert, and my brother, Levi Seibert, for reviewing this book and helping me edit it. Thanks to Levi as well for designing the cover and helping me publish *The Choice*.

PREFACE

I can never remember what first inspired my love for the history of the American Civil War. Maybe it was walking up the slopes of Little Roundtop, or perhaps it was watching the movie *Gettysburg*, or even living as close to Antietam as I did growing up. Regardless, the Civil War has held a strange fascination for me as long as I can remember. It was one of the bloodiest conflicts of our history, but it is perhaps one of the most misunderstood.

Though the majority of individuals think the war was over head-strong plantation owners who refused to recognize the dignity of human life, the true roots of the conflict run much deeper. Yes, slavery was a major part of the issues, but it was only that: a part. Political infighting, westward expansion, and changing economic climates, to name a few, all had their own role to play in the narrative.

Adding yet another level of interest to the study, some of the greatest generals and soldiers ever produced by America lived, fought, and died in the Civil War. Men like U. S. Grant, J. E. B. Stuart, William T. Sherman, Thomas (Stonewall) Jackson, and Robert E. Lee to just name a few. Many of these men had such internal struggles themselves which I found completely fascinating.

Throughout the years as I watched movies, visited battlefields, and read books, my fascination continued to grow. However, I began to notice two characteristics that marked so much of what I had studied and watched. First, almost without exception, all of the movies and books I read about the subject contained plenty of cursing and profanity—which I know was accurate to what happened, but unwholesome none the less. Second, nearly all the characters in the stories were fully persuaded one way or the other about the war, none truly seeming to wrestle within themselves about the "rightness" of either side.

So I began to consider, What would it have been like for a young man to live in the South, but still feel an obligation of loyalty to the North? And also, how could I present this in a wholesome, edifying manner? As I considered these two questions, I began to write this book, the first of a trilogy that traces the life of a young man from before the war, through the bloody conflict, and into the reconstruction period beyond.

This is by no means a textbook of events during the 1860s, but I have sought to preserve historical accuracy in these books. For example, I read numerous source documents and books and tried to imitate the vocabulary and syntax of how individuals spoke during that time. I also consulted several actual textbooks to ensure I was accurately reflecting the attitudes and events of the conflict. The major sources I consulted for these books include the following:

- Alice Williamson Diary. Duke University Special Collections, 1864.
  https://library.duke.edu/rubenstein/scriptorium/williamson/
- Shelby Foot. *The Civil War, Volumes 1-3, Random House, 1958.*
- Oxford University. *Battle Cry Of Freedom,* Oxford University Pres, 1988.
- *The Portable American Realism Reader, Kindle Edition,* Edited by James Nagel and Tom Quirk, Penguin Group, 1997.

- Leander Steelwell. *The story Of A Common Soldier, Franklin-Hudson Publishing, 1920.*
- Harriet Beecher Stowe. *Uncle Tom's Cabin, Viking Penguin Inc, 1850, 1981.*
- Samuel R. Watkins. *Company Aytch, Harper Collins, 2014.*

In addition to these books, I also talked with reenactors about life during this period, and checked my findings with several websites:

*Bennet Historic Site.
http://www.bennettplacehistoricsite.com/education/programs/on-the-homefront-during-the-civil-war/
* Learn North Carolina.
http://www.learnnc.org/lp/editions/nchist-antebellum/5334
* Nellaware.
http://www.nellaware.com/blog/civil-war-army-organization-and-order-of-rank.html
* U. S. History.
http://www.ushistory.org/us/34d.asp
*Visit Gettysburg.
https://www.visit-gettysburg.com/civil-war-clothes.html

While I have striven to maintain historical accuracy in this series, the characters and the individual events of their private lives are fictitious, though they are representative of actual groups of people who lived during the Civil War. With that said, however, all of the major events and dates involving the war are real.

I do not pretend to set forth in this book the "right"

decision that should have been made in this period of history. The choices that the individual characters make are simply that: their own choices. Some stubbornly follow their own will, yet others continually pour out their heart to the Father as they seek His will for their lives. I desire that as you read, you will be challenged to look to the Lord and follow wherever He leads in your own life, even if you are never faced with a decision as weighty as the ones Peter Brenton and his companions encounter. Jesus Christ is Lord over all of life, no matter how insignificant part of it may seem. May God bless you as you follow the journey of Peter Brenton and his comrades as they encounter *The Choice*.

Luke Seibert
August 2018
www.lukeseibert.com

CHAPTER ONE

The lathe wheel whirred upon the axle as Peter Brenton worked the foot petal up and down, continuing to carve the rotating table leg with his chisel. The partially complete oaken table lay upside down upon a faded quilt on the barn floor, its three finished legs pointing like church spires into the air. A few more strokes of the skew chisel, and Peter removed his foot from the petal and permitted the machine to slow to a stop. He replaced the chisel alongside its companions resting in the poplar cabinet above and to his right. The chisels were not new, but they were still in a tolerable condition. They would accomplish the purposes Peter needed, and had been offered in his allowable price range.

With the lathe having ceased its rotating, Peter removed the table leg from the machine's clamps and examined his work with an admiring gaze, raising it to the inspection of the light cascading through the open barn window fifteen feet above. Though he was not a vain man, his honest blue eyes approved of the examined object. It was the best one of this set. With a slight nod of satisfaction, the nineteen-year-old turned toward the table still lacking its final parts. "Yes sir, Henry. I dare say this will work." The boy—Henry—sat perched upon the maple workbench, contently munching on an apple that did not require significant number of bites to be reduced to its mere core. A handsome lad of eight, Henry sat with his small-visored cap pulled snuggly upon his dark head of curls, a gleam of boyish energy flickering in his green eyes. He wore a cotton shirt with the uppermost buttons unfastened, and his legs, swinging gently back and forth under the work bench, sported a pair of knickers which had obviously not originated with him.

"You done good, Peter. Looks mighty fine." Peter smiled warmly upon the young lad passing judgement on his craftsmanship. His youthful gaiety and propensity to trust had endeared the little fellow to him ever since his move to Chesson fourteen months previously. A few days after he took possession of the cabin, a buggy had drawn up in front of his porch from which a middle-aged gentlemen and a young boy had descended. It had been Henry, along with his father, Charles Taylor. The Taylors owned the farm abutting his own twenty acre parcel, and these two representatives of the family had called to welcome him to the community.

The Taylors were not a wealthy family—especially when compared with his own relatives—but they were greatly respected in the valley. Mr. Taylor owned a 200 acre farm which consumed most of his and his family's energy, yet he also ran a mill on the North side of his property. It was an added source of income for their family, and was greatly utilized by the surrounding farms. While not known as open abolitionists, Peter's neighbors felt quite strongly that it was inconsistent with their faith to own another human being. They did employ several servants and hired hands, but all were free Negro men and women.

Peter laid the table leg upon the much used workbench top, and reached behind his young companion for a drill lying alongside its case of bits. Henry watched with earnest interest as Peter chose a particular bit and secured it in the chuck of the drill. "Peter, how is it that ya remember which bit to choose? I can't hardly work my figures, no matter how often I read them in my book."

"Oh, you will get used to it." He tightened the chuck with a final twist. "After you do anything for a significant period of time, you just find that you remember it. Don't trouble yourself about this. But about your figures—what are you finding difficult about them?"

"I's just cannot keep all 'dem numbers straight. They's all just a'piling up inside my mind." The boy shook his head in an attitude of exasperation.

Peter aligned the drill bit with the intended hole, and began to rotate the crank handle, applying pressure with his other hand upon the top of the tool. "Well, have you asked Jenny to help you in the evenings after supper?"

Henry made a face and stuck out his tongue in feigned disgust. "Sir, when you have to put up with my sister in school all day, you would not request her help at home either." Jenny was Henry's eighteen-year-old sister, and also served as Chesson's teacher in their small, one-room school house. She had assumed the position after Mr. Silas Banks, the former schoolmaster, moved his family further south in consideration of his wife's health. She had a poor constitution, and the cold Virginia winters only aggravated her frequent ailments.

"Henry, you make it seem as though sisters were something despised and needed to be avoided as much as possible. They are not. I have always been close to my sister Olivia her whole life."

"I ain't saying I don't like her. It's just that when your sister is the teacher, you're expected to be smarter than all the other boys and make better grades."

Peter removed the drill from the hole he had created in the leg, and commenced drilling another one a little to the left of the original. "Well, if you would ask Jenny for help, I'm sure you would do better. I do not consider it a guarantee that you will be perfect, but I am assured you make more sense of your lessons. And," he looked up from his work with a wry smile, "if you didn't hang out over here so much, but applied yourself to your studies more, that would be a good beginning."

"Oh, Peter. You know us boys hate school." Henry chucked the apple core through the parted barn doors a few paces away. "I love watching you work. I want to be a cabinetmaker when I grow up, just like you."

"What would your father say about that? He needs your help on the farm with tending the fields, or helping at the mill as you grow into a young man."

"Oh, Pa's got William, James, and John to help him. And ain't you forgetting Tom and old man Zirus?"

Peter replaced the tool. "You had better not let your teacher hear you talking that'a way, or you'll receive an earful about the proper way to speak English."

"I'm sorry. I keep forgetting. It's not easy to always have to remember all this stuff they teach ya in school."

"I know, but as you continue to study and work at your lessons, you will find them easier to remember. Come here; you could hold this leg in position while I secure it in place."

Henry wiped his hands on his knickers and shoved himself off the bench. He grasped the table leg that Peter had placed firmly in its corner of the table, while Peter knelt with a few screws in his one hand and a screwdriver in the other. As he inserted the screws into their respective holes and tightened them with the tool in his hand, his young companion continued to watch with rapt attention. Once the screws were properly tightened, Peter rose on one knee, tested the stability of the leg with a gentle shake, and nodded in response to its resistance to his touch.

"Thank you for helping me today, Henry. I was really getting tired of that old crate I had gotten from the General Store that I was using as a table."

"You're welcome. I always enjoy watching you work. Besides, it's wash day today, and you know how Ma is when it comes to cleaning: if you are going to scrub the clothes, let's scrub the whole house." Peter playfully slapped the back of the boy's head.

"You little sneak, getting out of work by running over here. I've half a mind to turn you in."

"Please don't, Peter. Ma didn't say I *couldn't* spend the morning over here. To tell the truth, she asked me to come over."

Peter's brow furrowed slightly. "Asked you? Because you were getting in her hair and acting like an annoying mosquito?"

Henry was unable to determine whether the young man's remark was a rebuke, or simply playful banter. Even though he had five older brothers, he still looked up to Peter almost as if he was part of the family. He longed to find approval in his eyes, and would pass as many hours as he could watching the young man work on projects in the small barn on Saturdays. Peter worked with Mr. Samuel Kouffers during the week, employed in the older man's cabinet shop. But on Saturdays, Peter pursued his own work—either small tasks for neighbors and friends, or simply honing his woodworking skills with diligent practice.

Peter saw the consternation marked upon the other's face and put his fears to rest. "Henry, I'm only messing with you. I appreciate and enjoy having you spend time with me. I value your friendship, and you give me someone to talk to while I work. But seriously now, what did your mother send you over here for?"

The Choice

"Thank you, Peter." Relief swept over his round face. "I enjoy spending time with you, also. But I forgotten what Ma said until just now. She wants ya to come up to the house for supper tonight. Will ya come?"

"I suspect so, for I do not have any other plans this evening. I had some left over cornbread I was going to eat, but that'll keep till tomorrow."

"Fine. Ma's said we'd be having some pork chops and some turnips tonight, and I think a little corn also."

Peter strode toward a tall, slender cabinet opposite his workbench, Henry at his heels. "I'll be looking forward to that. Shawna's pork chops are always excellent." Shawna was the cook employed by the Taylors, but did not exclusively serve in that office. Mrs. Taylor and her daughter Jenny often would engage themselves in preparing the evening meal, but mostly it was Shawna's responsibility to fulfill that role.

The Taylor's stead lay only about a mile distant from Peter's cabin, and he would often walk along the lane and spend an evening with his amiable neighbors. As much as he enjoyed the time passed with his friends, he thoroughly enjoyed his solitary walks between the two houses. He had never been a very outgoing character, instead appreciating quiet moments in serene settings which afforded him opportunities for meditation and serious contemplation. He had a deep love for the scenes of nature that the Creator had made as if by the stroke of a painter's brush in the hand of a master artist—yet only more perfect. Many were the afternoons he would meander through the rolling hills, reveling in the surrounding beauty of first the towering oaks and hickories, next the murmuring streams babbling their way across rocky creek beds, and then the acres of open farmland wherein lay plots of cotton, tobacco, and wheat.

And that afternoon was not an exception to his former habit. Though Henry babbled the entirety of their walk, Peter continued with a steady, easy stride, an attitude of contentment about his manner. The weather was glorious that afternoon. September was drawing nigh to its end, and though the nights were progressively growing colder, the rising sun would warm the day to an affable temperature. Peter loved the autumn. It brought out such striking, vibrant colors in the leaves of the deciduous trees in his valley, and he could work all day without perspiring uncontrollably as he did in the summer's oppressive heat.

The tranquility of the walk immediately ceased upon their arrival at the Taylor's. Henry's next older brother—Robert—responded to his knock upon their door, inviting his neighbor and brother to enter. Upon crossing the threshold, Peter at once found himself feeling the atmosphere of joy that always pervaded the Taylor's home. Though John, their oldest son, had already married and settled with his wife, Sarah, in their own home three years ago, the Taylor's other eight children all still remained at home.

"Evening, Massa' Peter," greeted Loressa as she laid the proper settings upon the white table cloth. At fourteen years of age, she was Shawna's oldest daughter, and would dutifully assist her mother in many of the household tasks. She was instructing the Taylor's youngest child, Emily, on the proper order of the silverware at each place.

"Evening, Loressa," Peter nodded in return. "I hear your mother is cooking some pork chops for supper tonight."

"Ya hears right. Mama's got 'em on now and 'del be done right quick." Turning to her pupil, "That's right, Emily: spoon and knife on de right, fork on de left."

Six year old Emily smiled broadly at the praise, her auburn curls bouncing upon her little shoulders as her head bobbed excitedly. "Thank you, Lessa." No matter how many times her family tried to correct her, she could never quite make out "Loressa" always dropping the "or." But what she lacked in some of her pronunciation, she more than made up for in her energy. It always amazed Peter how she could suddenly appear out of nowhere one minute, and be off occupied in another task the next.

"That looks fine, Emily," encouraged Peter as he followed Henry to where his brothers, Robert and George, sat engaged in a game of cards in the adjacent sitting room. At least, the "sitting room" was the name they had bestowed upon the small edition to their home which contained a few rocking chairs lining the walls in pairs, a small side table in between many of them. A stone fireplace figured prominently in the midst of the longest wall, equally dividing the number of chairs on either side. As the duo entered, George, who faced the opening towards the table, acknowledged their arrival with a quick smile, "Evening, Peter." Then turning upon his youngest brother, "And where've ya been all day? Ma had us scrubbin' down the whole house, and Shawna helped us today—so it was even worse."

Peter rested his shoulder upon one of the supporting posts that designated the border of each room, anticipating how his young friend would save his marred reputation in his brother's eyes. George wasn't usually harsh, but since he turned fourteen, he had been assuming more of the role of a man, leaving his boyish playfulness behind.

Henry plopped into a wicker chair beside Robert, lifted his cap and scratched his shock of dark curls. Shrugging off the implied accusation of his negligence, he replied, "I's just over at Peter's helping him with that table he's been a'workin' on."

"You and your everlastin' love of building," sighed George exasperatedly, his eyes—along with his attention—returning to the game at hand. "I tell ya- I can't see what so fascinating about it. No disrespect, Peter. It's just not the boot that fits me, ya know?"

"I understand," returned Peter. "William back yet?"

Robert piped up, "Naw. He, James, and Pa had a few orders up at the mill they lacked, and had a mind to fill 'em before supper. They said they'd be along directly."

"Fine. I just knew that your brother wouldn't miss a meal of Shawna's pork chops," Peter chuckled.

"Oh, you can bet on that. He's about drove Ma and Shawna crazy, the way he's always swiping food to pack in his knapsack."

The door opened then and a bright, cheerful voice of a young lady burst upon the occupants of both rooms. "I'm home, Ma. Sorry I'm late."

Peter turned about to face the newcomer, and found Jenny untying the strands of her yellow bonnet, dulled by hours of exposure under the burning rays of the summer sun. Jenny removed the bonnet, revealing a quantity of light blonde hair tied in a neat bun. Her forehead glistened with the perspiration from her rapid return to the house. Laying her bonnet upon the shelf above the hat rack adjacent to the door, she turned and caught sight of Peter's presence. A charming, radiant smile spread across her face, accenting her cheeks rosy with her recent exertion. "Hello, Peter! I didn't know you would be joining us for supper. Of course, you are always welcome; we always enjoy your company."

"Thank you, Jenny. I consider it a privilege to be allowed to join your family with such frequency. Indeed, I consider it a true honor."

Jenny giggled, "Peter—you're doing it again." A middle aged woman in a simple cotton dress died a brownish hue appeared from the opposite hallway, and her quick ear caught the end of the young woman's remark.

"Evening, Peter. I am glad you are able to join us." Before the young man could form a reply, she turned towards her daughter and inquired, "But what's he done now?"

"Oh, not much. He just lapsed into his high society speech again, Ma." And then to her reddening neighbor, "I'm only kidding, Peter. You can talk how you please. But Chesson is not like the great cities; you don't have to be so formal."

"I know. Pard...pardon me. I just lapse into it without thinking sometimes, such as when someone pays me a compliment." It had taken Peter quite an amount of training to learn to lay aside the rigid formalities he had been raised with. Take, for example, his attitude toward Jenny Taylor. When he had first arrived in the Chesson community, he had instinctively referred to her as Miss Taylor. It was the proper way for a young man to refer to a young lady. And though the Taylors had encouraged him frequently to just call all of them by their given names, it had felt like learning an entire new culture to him. But he had conquered his reservations. It had taken time, but he did feel the freedom to be at his ease around his neighbors. That is, when there were no other parties present.

The door burst open once more, and three men— two younger, one middle aged—appeared in its wake. The oldest of the trio, a stocky fellow of no more than 5'

7", strode to Mrs. Taylor and wrapped her in a tender embrace. "Oh, Mary. Evening, my dear." And as he released her, "What's fer supper?"

"Charles Taylor—you had better learn that when you are greeting your wife after a long day, the first thing out of that mouth of yern had better not be about food."

"Pardon me, sweetheart. I'm forgetting my manners. How was your day?"

While Mary Taylor informed her husband of her exploits and accomplishments, the youngest of the new arrivals sprang to Peter's side, his outstretched hand preceding him. "Hey, Pete! Didn't know you's a'joining us tonight."

Peter gripped the firm hand and returned William Taylor's beaming grin. At twenty years of age, William was just a year older than Peter, and had grown into a sturdy young man with an honest gaze and a strong arm. Thin as a rail, but perpetually jubilant, he seemed to leap everywhere he went.

"Yeah, Henry spent most of the day with me, and your Mother asked if I would join you. Naturally, I consented." William slapped him on the shoulder. "Glad you could join us. Always, always enjoy your company."

Peter chuckled a warm, husky laugh. "Will, you keep saying that, but you don't need to continue repeating yourself. I know that I am welcome, and I avail myself of your family's hospitality at least twice a week."

"Sorry," he grinned sheepishly. "I do say it a little too much I suppose. But it does not change the fact that it's true."

"I know, and that is why I appreciate it."

The other boy who had entered with William joined him beside Peter and also offered his extended hand. "Evening, Pete."

"Evening, James. How were things at the mill today?"

"Tolerable. Busy, though. Had a lot of orders to fill for some wheat flour. I'm not complaining, we could always use the work."

"I understand."

The scraping of a spatula against a frying pan directed the young men's attention to the table, where Shawna had appeared, serving pork chops, collards, and sweet corn on every plate. "Ya'll come 'eat dis up while it's hot, hear? Don't make me have worked all afternoon for nuthin'."

■■■

"...she seemed to need someone to be with her today. I was glad I was able to go." They had finished the wonderful meal and had gathered in the sitting

room, each settling into a seat that sui
prepared to pass the remainder of the
relaxation and shared accounts of the d
completing her retelling of her time with
Mullins who lived a few plots over. Mrs.
her early eighties, and her husband had passed on about five or six years before Peter had arrived in the valley. She was a dear acquaintance of the Taylors, especially of Jenny. Although Mary could satisfactorily complete a patch job, the widow Mullins far outranked her as a seamstress, and Jenny would often pass an afternoon at her house either receiving instruction on various sewing techniques, or simply offering a listening ear to the widow's stories. Now that Jenny had started teaching school, her time with the widow was vastly limited compared to its earlier condition, yet she still eagerly seized any opportunity to visit the older woman.

"I'm pleased to hear that you were able to be an encouragement to her," commented her father. "Carson Jones was in today at the mill askin' 'bout when we might be able to grind up a load of barley for him. I told him it be another week, just 'bout, but we'd see to it quick as we could." The full-bearded man settled back against his rocker, a slow, heavy sigh escaping his parted lips. "And that's not all he was talkin' about, neither."

Not looking up from her needle work, his wife quarried, "Oh? What was he wanting? Some more help on his land?"

"No, they are not. We are not guaranteed any rights in this life, James. We cannot demand to have things our way. Remember our Lord, who even though he existed in the form of God, 'thought it not robbery to be equal with God, but made himself of no reputation, taking the form of a servant. And being found in human form, he humbled himself and became obedient to the point of death, even the death of the cross.'"

"I understand, Father. It's just the North is so different than we are, it's as if they are their own nation already. I think it would make things so much easier if we were officially made into separate unions."

"What are your thoughts, Peter?" William interjected. He knew his father's views on the Union of the States, and he understood his elder brother's infatuation with the concept of a Southern nation. If they were left to themselves, he reasoned, no profit would result of the prolonged debate.

Peter never offered his opinions on anything freely, but especially not on political matters, and most certainly not in James' presence. James was quite emphatic in his view being the correct one and the only correct one. You either agreed with him, or else were in error in your reasoning. But at Charles' addition to William's request, he reluctantly began in his slow, thoughtful way, "Well...I would like to see an end of the tensions that have been building, but I don't know that separating would be the solution. I can see both sides, though. I am in agreement with you, sir," he nodded toward the older gentlemen, "in that I feel that the government in Washington should receive our submission and cooperation as good, loyal citizens. Yet, I don't know that there will ever be a reconciling of our radically different ways of life. And, I'm afeared of how far slavery might spread if the South does stay in the Union. First we had the Missouri compromise, but that was done away with. And now with Kentucky, Kansas and Nebraska being granted popular sovereignty on the issue of slavery, what is to stop any other state in the Union from being granted that privilege? If the South was to form its own country, at least slavery might be contained. I am just as much opposed to the institution as you all are, which you are aware of, and if I perceived that it could be done away with peaceably, I would resist any attempts to form a separate nation. Yet unfortunately, I fail to see a path that would seem to work. One may very well exist, but the ones that I have heard explained do not appear to present a practical plan that would actually accomplish the desired result."

"Thank you, Peter," James slapped his knee. "This is my point. We cannot stay in the Union—"

"James, we both know how the other feels, and this is not edifying to any of us here if we continue this disagreement any further. I respect your opinion, but you must respect my authority as the head of this house."

"Bu...yes sir," James returned, but from his set jaw and the fire flickering in his passionate eyes, Peter knew the matter was far from settled.

CHAPTER TWO

In a voice that filled the one-room, lap board structure, Reverend Daniels finished the concluding prayer of the service. "...we ask all these things, Father, in the most blessed, holy name of Thy Son, Jesus Christ. Amen." As the congregation lifted their heads which had previously been bowed in reverence for the prayer, the pastor smiled warmly on the families gathered in the pews before him. "May the Lord bless you all this coming week. You are dismissed."

Peter rose from the hard wooden pew, straightening his suit jacket as he drew himself to his full height and surveyed the room. Chesson's church was not large compared to the one he had attended during his childhood, but it was a substantial building for the families that lived in the valley. The truth be told, many of the families considered it a true blessing to have a building to gather in as a church that was separate from the school house a short walk down the street, since many other communities could not even afford that.

"Fine sermon, was it not?" a husky voice remarked from behind his right shoulder.

Turning towards the aisle, Peter found himself confronted by the smiling figure of his employer, Samuel Kouffers. Broad shouldered and deep chested, Samuel possessed a commanding appearance, yet his kindly eyes and gentle smile revealed his true heart of compassion. He had long since moved past his self-consciousness of his receding hairline. "I'm sixty-two, and ain't getting any younger," he explained to Peter one day while working upon a cabinet. "I might as well accept it, 'cause worring 'bout it won't change a thing." It was pieces of advice like that which Samuel would work into his conversations that had created the deep respect Peter had for the older man. Though Samuel was a master carpenter and taught Peter as fast as he could learn, it was the fitly spoken words and godly wisdom that he treasured most.

Peter reached out a hand and gripped Samuel's calloused one. "Yes sir, it was. His challenge to always speak the truth corresponded to my own studies in Proverbs 30, and how highly valued truthfulness actually is in a person's life."

"Ya can't put a price on honesty, son. Always remember that."

"Yes sir. I will."

Samuel glanced around the building's interior, and finding no one in their immediate vicinity, lowered his voice. "And speaking of truth...have you told them yet?"

Peter's eyes drifted downwards as he bit his lower lip in embarrassment. Without directly meeting Samuel's gaze, he replied, "No sir, I'm afraid I have not."

"Naw. He's all worked up again over states' rights. He gets into one of his moods ever so often, and expects everyone he meets to match his fervor."

Listening intently to the sudden change in conversation, James joined the recount of Jones' talk with eagerness. "He thinks things are getting quite heated up in Washington, and many of the states aren't takin' too kindly to it. South Carolina's threatening to secede—can you believe it?"

"They are doing what?" Mary was incredulous.

"He's right," agreed Charles reluctantly. "He was saying that the Senators are butting their stubborn heads together like two ornery ole mules, neither willin' to back down."

"And from what I hear tell, South Carolina ain't alone," his son continued. "Mississippi, Alabama—well, the whole cotton south really—they're all drawing more and more away from the idea that our differences can be worked out. I wouldn't be surprised if one day there might be the Southern States of America."

"James," Charles stern voice took on a note of reproach, "what kind of talk is that? We have no quarrel with the government in Washington. The President permits each citizen to worship the Lord as he sees fit, he protects us from the villains, and—"

"Except the villains in their fancy big houses up there with them who are workin' feverishly to take away our rights!"

room, each settling into a seat that suited him best, and prepared to pass the remainder of the evening in simple relaxation and shared accounts of the day. Jenny was completing her retelling of her time with the widow Mullins who lived a few plots over. Mrs. Mullins was in her early eighties, and her husband had passed on about five or six years before Peter had arrived in the valley. She was a dear acquaintance of the Taylors, especially of Jenny. Although Mary could satisfactorily complete a patch job, the widow Mullins far outranked her as a seamstress, and Jenny would often pass an afternoon at her house either receiving instruction on various sewing techniques, or simply offering a listening ear to the widow's stories. Now that Jenny had started teaching school, her time with the widow was vastly limited compared to its earlier condition, yet she still eagerly seized any opportunity to visit the older woman.

"I'm pleased to hear that you were able to be an encouragement to her," commented her father. "Carson Jones was in today at the mill askin' 'bout when we might be able to grind up a load of barley for him. I told him it be another week, just 'bout, but we'd see to it quick as we could." The full-bearded man settled back against his rocker, a slow, heavy sigh escaping his parted lips. "And that's not all he was talkin' about, neither."

Not looking up from her needle work, his wife quarried, "Oh? What was he wanting? Some more help on his land?"

"I see," Samuel nodded slowly, a hint of disappointment appearing in his brown eyes. "Did you not have a chance to speak with them this week?"

"No sir, it was not that. It's..." his voice trailed off as he searched for an explanation, an explanation that was successfully eluding him since it did not exist.

Giving the young man a moment to collect his thoughts, Samuel prodded, "I thought we had discussed this all a few days ago and you agreed that it was time to tell the Taylors."

"We did. I know I should have already done it a long time ago, as you had said, but I...I am at a loss for how I can reveal the truth to them."

"Son, they have taken you in, shown you true Christian fellowship, and been your faithful friends whenever you have needed them. They will not treat you differently or judge you if you tell them. They need to know, and after all they have done for you since you moved here, you certainly owe them nothing short of the truth."

Peter lifted his eyes to meet the steady gaze of his older friend. The eyes were firm, yet tender to Peter's predicament. He knew that Samuel was only exhorting him out of love and a desire to see him grow into a mature man, characterizations that had marked so many of their conversations since he had arrived in Chesson.

"You are right, sir," Peter conceded. "I should have long since explained my situation to them, but I give you my word, I will settle things with them this week. Mr. and Mrs. Taylor at least, anyway."

"Good. How 'bout you make it this afternoon or tomorrow?"

"Sir?"

"Peter," the man smiled gently, "the longer we put off carrying out our resolutions, the more of a foothold that old snake the Devil tightens his hold upon us and cripples our determination. Do not waste any more time than is necessary. I can understand your not wanting to explain everything in front of the whole family all at once, but I urge you to talk with Charles and Mary as soon as you are able."

"I will, sir. I will speak with them."

"Very well," Samuel nodded, slapping the young man's shoulder. "I will be praying for you. I have been, but I will continue to do so even more."

"Thank you, sir. I truly appreciate that."

"We are called to encourage one another, and we must seek to always spur one another on as we grow in the Lord."

"Speaking of growth," a tall, well-dressed man in his early forties approached the pair. "Tensions are growing more and more heated with each passing day, and if you ask me, something is fixin' to happen."

With a friendly tone which only slightly revealed the affectedness of its nature, Samuel returned as he shook the newcomer's hand, "And how are you this morning, Jones?"

"Doing well. I—"

"You know, I was just telling Peter how it is such a blessing to see how the Lord works through His children, how He grows them ever more into the image of His Son: don't you agree?"

Annoyance flickered momentarily in Carson Jones' eye, then faded as his expression resumed its normal passionate manner. Peter had only limited exposure to the man, but from experience and from what other men had told him, Carson was always ready to either vehemently argue or defend any given topic, but especially those dealing with state's rights.

"To be sure, it is," Carson concurred. "People change all the time. They may be adamantly against something one day, but give them a little time to think it through and—"

"Jones," Samuel raised a hand in interruption, "I have not, and will not change my mind about your political ideas. If fellas like you have your way, then so be it. Only be sure that I will have no part in it. How is that new Jersey you picked up last month; she milkin' well?"

"Tolerable enough, thank you. I think's she about dried up though, so I'll have to wait till spring to know for sure." His eye drifted towards those filing through the back doors of the building. "Hey Mason," he called after a man retrieving his hat from the rack he had deposited it upon. "Excuse me, Kouffers, Peter," Carson took his leave and strode to the man he had hailed.

Samuel shook his head slowly as he turned back to face Peter. "That man is something else, ya know it?"

"Yes sir. He seems to have a way with getting people worked up over so many issues. Just the other day, he had James Taylor going on again about state's rights."

"Mmpph. And what did Charles say to that?"

"I was only there when it came up in the evening at supper, but Mr. Taylor firmly resisted any talk of secession."

"That is what I figured. Oh Peter," he sighed, "things keep getting worse and worse. I keep telling myself they are going to get better, but this rift that has started only seems to be growing wider." He glanced up at the young man. "What am I doing, carrying on like this on today of all days. We can talk about all that some other time. On a different note, I received a letter from Nathan yesterday."

Nathan Lee was Samuel's eldest grandson, living in South Carolina with his family. He and his grandfather exchanged letters with much frequency, and Samuel had often mentioned Peter in his replies to the notes received from Nathan. Peter did not know the young man very much, but from the time they had passed together during a visit Nathan had made to his grandparents earlier in the spring, Peter had been intrigued by his character and personality.

"Is that so? How does he find himself these days?"

"He wrote that he and the family were doing well. There was not much of news in what he said, but he did mention that he desired to pay us another visit before long."

"That is wonderful; I know you and your wife must be excited to see him again."

Samuel smiled warmly. "That we are, son. That we are. He also wrote that he was looking forward to meeting you again. Apparently, you made quite the impression upon him during his last visit, and he has been eagerly anticipating his journey to Chesson."

"I am honored he should remember me in that way. Nathan made a deep impression upon me this spring as well, and I enjoy hearing you share about him and his letters. He strikes me as a godly young man who lives a steadfast and honest life."

"Well, the boy comes from good stock," Samuel commented, a twinkle in his eye.

"Yes sir, I dare say he does," Peter returned, a short laugh escaping from his throat.

"Excuse me," chuckled Samuel, wagging his head. "I do not mean to sound vain. Alma asked me earlier, and I forgot to mention it to you before service, but we would be honored if you would join us for dinner. Unless you have other plans..." a knowing look crept into his eye.

Peter glanced at Charles Taylor passing through the rear door of the church with the last of his family preceding him. "No sir, I do not have any plans." He turned back to face Samuel. "I am obliged to you for the offer. I can accomplish the other matter tomorrow evening after work."

Samuel nodded. "Very well. I will tell the wife, and then we will be ready to go."

■■

Peter laid the soapstone upon the ground beside the bench he was kneeling before and ran a hand over the rounded edge of the seat. It could use a little more sanding, he decided, and resumed rubbing the stone in long strokes along the top-most board's edge. From as far back as his memory contained record of, he had always been fascinated by the ability of carpenters he had seen who could make beautiful moldings and furniture from simple, plain boards sawed from the hardwoods around his family's home. He had not received any opportunities to learn the trade as a boy, and it was not until he had begun work under Samuel that he had learned even the most basic knowledge of a craftsmen.

But as limited as Peter's knowledge and experience were, Samuel Kouffers' ability as a carpenter more than made up for any lack of skill on the young man's part. Samuel was well known as one of the finest cabinetmakers in the whole valley—that part of Virginia, even—and had a steady flow of employment. It had not taken Peter much time to learn to accomplish the simplest tasks of woodworking, and as his employer recognized his ability to comprehend and learn new methods and skills, he quickly progressed as a qualified apprentice.

As Peter completed a final stroke on the board's edge, he ran his fingers once again along the profile of the bench. Satisfied with the smoothness of its surface, he pushed himself up with his other hand and strode over to the work table where Samuel was sketching out a curve on a strip of hickory. "I believe I have finished that bench, Mr. Kouffers. What would you have me to do now, sir?" Samuel finished the last arc of the curve he had started marking, then raised his eyes to meet Peter's.

"You believe it is finished? Is it finished, or ain't it?" It wasn't a rebuke, simply a question to test Peter's confidence in his work.

"It is finished," Peter smiled. Recently, Samuel had been trying to help Peter overcome his natural timidity, but as fast as Peter was in learning a skill with his hands, changing his mindset—like his vocabulary—was a slow, tedious task.

Samuel nodded. "Alright. You recall the finish we used for the other part of the set, correct?"

"Yes sir."

"So, while I finish markin' these boards, go ahead and apply the finish to the bench."

"Yes sir."

Peter retrieved the can of stain Samuel had designated and the two men returned their attention to their respective tasks. Admiring the deep, ruddy tones of the wood's grain that the stain drew out, Peter smoothly wiped the damp rag across the boards of the bench. He glanced at the lengthening shadows the sinking sun cast through the two windows of the shop, realizing that the time was fast approaching when they would cease their work for the day. Though he usually wished to work as long as Samuel would allow, he desired to be finished with the day's tasks, yet it was not from any eagerness of what came afterwards. The truth be told, it was the exact opposite.

Tightening the lid back upon the jar, Peter rose from his squatted position and strode to replace the finish in its cabinet. Setting it upon its shelf, he turned to face Samuel, who was examining the bench.

With a nod of satisfaction, Samuel remarked. "That looks fine. I think we will go ahead and call it a day."

"Yes sir," Peter acknowledged, untying his leather apron.

"You going to talk with Charles?"

Peter stopped with his hand upon the rack they hung their coats upon. "Yes sir, I am stopping by the mill on my way home this evening."

"Do not worry about it, son. Speak the truth, that is all you have to do."

"I am not worried," Peter confessed, turning around, "only nervous—nervous of what they might say."

"You have nothing to fear. They know you, they know your character. You have chosen to follow the Lord, and they recognize that in your life. Let the truth be known. The Lord will bless you for it."

"Thank you, sir."

"Good evening, Peter."

"Evening. See you in the morning." He stepped through the shop's open door and began his journey towards his home.

He could not fully explain himself to Samuel, but it was not Charles' reaction that mostly concerned him. It had at one point, but he had moved past that. What unsettled Peter was choosing how to start his explanation. He had never been good with words, especially when uncomfortable, and his peculiar habit of lapsing into a formal manner of speaking evidenced the fact. He had wrestled with finding the right words, but he could never settle upon one statement that was better than another, so in resignation to his task, he had chosen to simply begin at the beginning and tell everything to the Taylors. The older ones, that is. Henry and Emily's mouths moved too freely for Peter to be comfortable with them knowing what he had to say. He would tell them one day, but not then.

Nearing his destination, the low, moaning rumble of a millstone turning on its axel wafted through the air to meet him. He stepped up into the open doorway and rapped against the worn doorframe. William was occupied in lashing an end closed on a sack of grain, while his father sat hunched over his desk with his back towards the door and James poured more grain In between the millstones.

William raised his head at the knock, and his eyes, dulled by the monotony of his task, burst with recognition when they rested on his friend. Jumping up from his task, he cried jubilantly, "Hey, Pete! What cha doing out this way this afternoon? Come in, come in!"

Peter smiled softly at his neighbor's enthusiasm and accepted the invitation. "Thank you, William. Afternoon, James, Mr. Taylor."

"Afternoon, Peter," James responded, supplementing the greeting with a friendly nod of the head.

His father turned away from the log books he had ben scrutinizing and rose to meet his neighbor with an outstretched hand. "Peter, good to see you, my boy. How do you find yourself this fine day?"

"I am well, thank you. And yourself?"

"Tolerable. Work's been pouring in here left and right, and I'm finding it quite difficult to break away to make sure my fields are tended to properly, getting them ready for winter and all that. However, I am grateful for the Lord's provision He has given us. What can I do for you this evening?"

"Well...I was wanting to talk with you about something, something I should have told you already."

Charles' face creased with concern while his sons exchanged furtive glances with one another. "I trust nothing serious has happened," Charles remarked slowly.

"No sir, it is not something that has happened. It is only that—"

Another rap sounded upon the door post and the mill's occupants turned to find a tall young man stepping inside. The new comer was young, about Peter and William's age, the oldest son of another neighboring farm, Seth Mason. The Masons were closely connected with the Jones family, and as emphatic as that man could be, Seth was even more passionate in his views. A tall, strapping man of nearly 6' 1", his broad shoulders and well cut features only added to his handsome appearance—a fact he was well aware of. Peter had met Seth shortly after moving to

Chesson, but even from that first meeting, there was something about him that unsettled Peter. He couldn't put his finger on exactly the issue. It wasn't his arrogance—though it often annoyed Peter to no end—nor was it his competitive spirit. There was always something about his manner and his eyes that seemed rascally to Peter. It was as if he always suspected some dark secret and was searching for any sign of what it might be.

Why did he have to come by now of all times, Peter inwardly groaned. He had almost found the words he needed to begin his explanation to Charles, but with Seth's arrival, the thoughts fled from his mind. It did not matter, though, since he was not going to continue his conversation with Seth within earshot.

"Excuse me," Charles whispered to Peter, then called, "How are you this evening, Seth?"

"Doing well, sir. Quite well."

"It's been quite a spell since you dropped by," James noted casually.

"I reckon it has been, but I've been busy with Pa and helping my uncle up at the store some. Anyway, Ma sent me up here for some barley flour, if'n ya'll had some set by already ground up, that is."

"I reckon we might have some," Charles nodded slowly. "I'll be right with you." He turned back to Peter. "Now, you were saying?"

"Uh, well," Peter coughed, his eyes drifting back towards Seth conversing easily with William by the doorway to the mill.

Recognizing Peter's dilemma, Charles called, "William, I think we might have a few sacks left over out on the side shed. Why don't you take Seth and see how many are there and if they will be enough for what he needs?"

"I think—" William started, but caught the silent communication in his father's eye. "—Yes sir, I think we have some out there. Come on, Seth." The two young men left the shop and Peter felt himself breathe a little easier.

Charles waited another moment before continuing. "Now, what is it, son? I assume it is a private matter?"

Nodding solemnly, Peter consented, "Yes sir, it is. I need to tell you where I truly came from.

CHAPTER THREE

A cold wind forcing its way through cracks in the barn wall caused Peter to shiver. Momentarily pausing his brushing of his horse Pat, he shook his shoulders once again and turned up his collar. Several weeks had passed since he disclosed to Charles Taylor his real background. He had never lied, yet had conveniently refrained from sharing certain details in their previous conversations. Hesitantly, he had explained that he had actually grown up on one of the richest plantations in their part of the state, coming from an influential family in high society. Perhaps it had been silly for him to think it was better to keep his past a secret, but every time he thought of his family's home, his heart filled with shame.

Still, a strange feeling had crept into his heart once he had finished his explanation, laying all the truth before Charles and James. They had been shocked at first, but as they considered it, they understood more of his peculiarities with their new knowledge of his upbringing. Charles had assured him that it changed nothing between them, just like Samuel had predicted. Before taking his leave that evening at the mill, Peter asked Charles to share the information with only his wife and William. Though he did not mind them knowing, he did not wish it to become common knowledge. Charles had promised to keep it among the older members of his family, and though he did not think Peter's fears were well founded, he understood his reasons.

With a final brush of the horse's coat, Peter sighed, "It's really starting' to feel like this winter will be a tough one, girl." The mares' blowing was the only reply. Peter affectionately slapped the horse's side. "Yeah, I know girl."

He replaced the brush on the nail he had partially driven into one of the posts by Pat's stall. Even though he had lived in Virginia his whole life, those first few weeks in November were always a struggle for him to adjust to the colder temperatures and damper conditions. But he never complained. Peter was not the sort of man to add to the burden of others by sharing his aggravations and annoyances to every listening ear. He bore what he had to, kept a stiff upper lip, and moved ahead with what he knew he must accomplish.

Peter retrieved a few ears of corn suspended from the rafters of the barn loft, then turned about on his way back towards the house, but halted when the sound of an approaching carriage arrested his attention. It was not the usual rubbing and clacking sound of a farm wagon, or even that of a small buggy.

He parted the barn doors and stepped out into the sunlight, his eyes searching for the distinct sounding vehicle. His soft green eyes lighted on a regal carriage with the hood up, decked out with fine riggings, and pulled by two magnificent black Thoroughbreds. He had seen this carriage before, yet the sight aroused a mixture of joy and anxiety in his heart: it was his family's coach.

As the carriage drew up in front of his small cabin, Peter approached with a hesitant step, unsure of what tidings awaited him upon his meeting of the newcomers. The driver, a Negro boy of about seventeen, leapt from the seat upon which he had perched and opened the carriage's door with a flourish, a wide grin forming upon his face as his eyes met those of Peter.

"Hello, Massa Peter!"

"Hello, Jethro," Peter returned, worry filling his voice. "How do you find yourself?"

"More den tolerable, sir."

"Jethro, what are you doing all the way up—"

"Well, I declare: that's a fine way to greet your sister!" A young lady lowered herself from the carriage, tossing her long, black curls as she smiled ruefully at Peter. "I had not expected these backwoods would have changed you so much that you have been deprived of all your manners." The girl was young, no more than sixteen years of age, yet an air of superiority pervaded her figure. She wore a long, flowing gown of fine fabric in a light blue hue, over which lay a dark fur coat. As she stood expectantly awaiting Peter's reply, a young man of a towering frame stepped out of the coach and placed himself at her side.

A look of consternation passed over Peter's face, and though his eyes remained wary, his expression softened into a welcoming smile as he gazed at his sister. "Olivia! It is so good to see you."

She laughed, "Well, I am glad to hear you say that, since I was beginning to wonder if you would ask me to get back in the carriage and drive off."

"No, I would never do anything of the sort. I was..." His voice trailed off as he took in the youth standing beside Olivia. He was well over a head taller than she was, yet seemed to be no more than a year or two her senior. The young man was of a tall build, broad in the shoulders which were nicely accentuated by the pristine, tailored traveling great coat he wore.

Observing the unvoiced question forming in Peter's eyes, Olivia announced, "Pardon me, now I am the one who has forgotten her manners. Peter, may I present Mr. Lawrence Johnston. Lawrence, this is my older brother, Peter Brenton."

Still unsure of what to make of Lawrence's presence, Peter reached out with his free hand and grasped the young man's offered one. "I am pleased to make your acquaintance, Mr. Johnston."

"The honor is mine. Your charming sister has often spoken of you with deep admiration and warmth, and I have looked forward to this meeting with much anticipation."

Peter hadn't the faintest notion of the meaning of Lawrence's comment. Who was this young man, and why had he and Olivia come to see him? Rubbing her small, white hands together, Olivia exclaimed, "Peter, it is positively freezing out here! Do you have a fire going inside this cabin of yours, or is that too sophisticated for a ruffian like you now?"

Realizing his inhospitable behavior, Peter shook himself and sprang towards the door. Pulling it open, he motioned for his sister and Lawrence to enter. The couple passed into the room and Peter turned toward Jethro, still standing erect by the coach. "Jethro, will you come inside?"

The servant boy grinned and shook his head slightly as he responded, "No sir, Massa Peter. My place is by the coach." A shadow briefly passed across Peter's face at Jethro's address. With his voice filled with solemnity, Peter corrected, "Jethro, do not call me that; I am not any man's master."

"Yes sir. Don't bother yourself about me; I am used to the cold, and it's not even really winter yet. I'll be fine."

Peter's face darkened with anger, but he waited for the ominous expression to dissipate before entering the cabin and closing the door softly behind him. He found Lawrence assisting Olivia in removing her wrappings, revealing the full elegance of her dress accented by lace trimmings at the neckline and the cuffs of the full, straight sleeves. Peter was struck with his sister's beauty; he had not realized how mature in age she had become. She was sixteen now, he realized—practically a woman. Another realization appeared in his mind as he watched Lawrence pull out a chair for Olivia: he was not the only one to have taken note of the attractiveness of his sister.

Peter pulled up one of the chairs to face the ones Olivia and Lawrence occupied by his fireplace. It had been nearly eight months since he had last seen anyone in his family, and Olivia had sent him no warning of her arrival. That, in conjunction with the presence of Lawrence whom she seemed to be on very friendly terms with, baffled him in no small way. As he lowered himself into the oak seat, Peter began, "Olivia, it is indeed good to see you. To what do I owe this unexpected pleasure?"

"Nothing in particular. It has been sometime since I have seen you, and Lawrence had a few days at his disposal, so we decided to pay you a surprise visit."

Alarm flooded Peter's mind. *They were here to stay for a few days? Surely Father had not approved of this plan.* "You…you said a few days?"

"Peter, don't trouble yourself!" Olivia giggled condescendingly. "We are not staying *here* for a few days. Lawrence was just staying at the house this weekend, thus it was the perfect time for such a visit as this. Drive up here in the morning, spend a few hours with you, and make it home before night fully sets in. You are so funny, Peter—the expressions you show. Did you honestly think I would ever spend a night in a place like this? I am sure it is adequate for you—you have changed so much—but I can never picture myself ever being disposed to accepting accommodations like this, can you, Lawrence?"

The look exchanged between the two young people only added to mounting concern within Peter. He attempted to direct the conversation along a more suitable path. "Tell me, Olivia: how is the rest of our family? It has been a while since I have received a letter from yourself or Mother."

Reluctantly tearing her eyes from the handsome Lawrence, Olivia answered, "Everyone is doing fine. Father has been preoccupied lately with the political situation. His Senator friends have taken up most of his time and attention. But you know that Father always finds something that vies for his time against the plantation. Mother conducts her regular circuit of calls each week, and I accompany her most times. I do not see why so many of the men are so concerned with what is happening in Washington; nearly all of the ladies see nothing to have raised such alarm, and life in general is continuing as it always has. And as busy as I was before, Lawrence has been taking me on drives and escorting me to balls—"

"You say that society life is continuing as usual," Peter cut in, checking the turn in conversation. He was not at all comfortable with the closeness of Lawrence to Olivia's side, nor the fondness with which she looked into his eyes. "Does the church still hold its annual relief banquet for the poor?"

Olivia turned an annoyed eye upon Peter and replied curtly, "Yes, of course Reverend Norton has us put on the banquet. Why does that concern you? You're not there to attend."

"I was only curious."

"Well, since you are so curious," Olivia continued, "I received a letter from cousin Esther last week. She wrote how she and Charlotte have been attending some of the great balls in Philadelphia…" She launched into a discussion of their influential cousins in Pennsylvania, a comparison of which gowns were the latest style, what new influences were coming to society, and other such topics that were of great interest to a sixteen year old girl in high society Virginian circles.

Although Peter found the monologue exceedingly droll, he was grateful that he had successfully drawn his sister into a topic that did not include the distinguished Lawrence Johnston. He listened attentively, trying to keep the conversation going by adding comments at lulls in Olivia's ramblings. The threesome continued their evaluation of societal life between the Northern states and those of the South for some time until Peter's ears picked up the sound of voices by the front door. The words were muted, but he still caught the tail end of them.

"…alone, Emily."

"I'll just let him know we brought 'em." A light knock sounded on the cabin door and Peter rose and quickly strode to answer. He opened the door and found little Emily Taylor smiling up at him. "Afternoon, Peter."

Peter returned the warm greeting, "Afternoon to you, Emily." Jenny joined her younger sister, flushing slightly with embarrassment. "Peter, I am so sorry. I told her not to knock, seeing's how you had company. We were just dropping off the eggs and milk like we usually do."

"It is fine, Je—" Peter caught himself and his smile morphed into a stoic solemnity. "Miss Taylor, do not trouble yourself about it. Please, will you and your sister come inside?"

"If you do not think we are intruding…" countered Jenny, curiosity at Peter's sudden change of demeanor painted across her forehead.

"It will not be an intrusion in the least. Please come in."

The two girls entered, Emily beaming, Jenny still uncertain. Peter made introductions between his neighbors and his sister and her apparent suitor, noting with shame the distain and contempt with which Olivia took in the simple, home-spun skirts of his young neighbors. Had he really been like this himself? He drew up a few more chairs for Jenny and Emily, but felt Olivia's eyes upon his every move. When he turned to face her, her eyes contained a note of mocking condescension.

He cleared his throat, "Um...Olivia, would you mind if I asked you to step outside with me for a moment?"

"Outside?" Mortification at the prospect filled her voice.

"Yes, please. It is important. Excuse us, Mr. Johnston, Miss Taylor."

With a huff of annoyance, Olivia drew her mantle about her and walked through the door as Peter followed.

"Can you please explain yourself? You are being impossibly rude. If you wanted to speak to me privately, why did you not ask those farm girls to step out here? They're used to the cold."

"Olivia, I need to talk with you without Mr. Johnston listening." She warily eyed him as she awaited his explanation.

"Does Father know about your traipsing all across Virginia with a young man, alone?"

"How dare you, Peter Brenton! What kind of woman do you think I am?"

"Olivia, hear me, it is not proper—"

"Not proper? How can you say anything about propriety? You live in a musty, damp cabin and treat farm girls better than your own sister!"

"Before you pass judgement on my neighbors, I want an answer about this young man, Lawrence

Johnston. What is he doing with you? You are barely sixteen, and Father should know that is way too young for a suitor to be pursuing your hand. He is taking far too many liberties with you, and I am shocked that Father would permit all this."

A smug grin of superiority grew upon Olivia's face. Folding her arms, she saucily quarried, "What makes you think that Father doesn't know?" In response to Peter's silence, she continued, "Father happens to think very highly of Lawrence, and it is well known in the neighborhood that he has begun a courtship with me."

Peter stood dumbfounded for a moment, unable to find words to express the shock he experienced at this revelation. *How could Father approve of this? Have I really come so far to think this improper?* "You mean to tell me that this young upstart has actually begun a courtship with—"

"Jenny."

The one word accompanied by the triumphant glow in Olivia's eyes cut Peter's rebuke mid-sentence. His brow furrowed and he rubbed his thumb against the fingers of his right hand. "What about Miss Taylor?"

"Oh, I saw you try to cover because I was there, but I still heard you start to call that young lady by her given name. Before you give me a verbal thrashing for my conduct, perhaps you would do well to examine your own."

Peter began to flush, but from a comprehension of his sister's meaning rather than from embarrassment. "I assure you that there is nothing between myself and Miss Taylor. I have become very close to her older brothers since I moved here and she has become like a younger sister to me. I consider her in a fashion similar to the way I view our relationship. I understand that it may appear that I have a double standard, but I do not. I have never been alone with any young lady, nor do I spend nights—days—at her family's house. You have to consider how young you are, Olivia. This Lawrence Johnston can hardly be much older than yourself— would it not be better to wait a few more years before considering a relationship?"

The two siblings continued to defend themselves against accusations of the other until Peter concluded that their conversation was not achieving anything, save that it was making Olivia even more aggravated with him. Their Father had passed judgement on the relationship, and nothing that Peter could say would change her mind, especially not with the quick exchange between Peter and Jenny Taylor at the cabin door.

They returned to the house and resumed their seats by the fireplace. Strained bits of conversation passed between the various members of the party until Olivia suggested that it was probably about time for her and Lawrence to begin the journey home. The pair dawned their heavy outer garments and took their leave of Peter, Jenny, and Emily. While his neighbors began gathering their things with in the cabin, Peter accompanied Olivia and Lawrence to the carriage.

The two Taylor girls joined Peter as he watched the coach roll down the lane, taking his sister and her suitor back to the plantation that was her pride and Peter's stigma of reproach in his heart. Concern knitted Jenny's brow as she asked, "Peter, are you well?"

"I will be fine. I did not know they were coming, and it took me by surprise. Forgive me for my somber attitude."

"No, forgive us for interrupting your company. I fear it was our entrance that caused her to leave."

"No, it was not you. I was the one who started the problem that brought about their departure."

"Well, regardless of who is responsible, I am sorry they left the way they did. But anyway, as I told you earlier, we put the eggs and milk in their place, and Ma said we have plenty more if you need them."

"Thank you very much, Jenny. Might I accompany you and Emily back to the house?"

"I fear we have imposed on you enough as it is. I cannot ask you to do that."

"No. Please allow me the opportunity; the walk will do me good."

The threesome commenced the nearly mile-long journey to the Taylor's home. Peter remained silent for a moment, then with a face communicating regret, turned to his companions. "I owe you two ladies an apology for what happened back there. It was instinctual for me to call you Miss Taylor around my sister. Whenever I am around people from my past, or people like them, I tend to lapse into speaking that same way. So, forgive me Jenny, for doing that.

"And Olivia was entirely out of line with her attitude and manner. If she knew you all, she would not have been so rude. My sister is infatuated in high society life, has been since as long as I can remember. You dangle any pretty, shiny thing in front of her, and she will run to it with all possible speed that she could muster. I am telling you this so that maybe you can understand her reasons for acting the way she did. I am not excusing her, but I owe you both an apology and an explanation."

"I forgive you," warmly encouraged Jenny, accompanying her words with an affirming smile. "To tell the truth, I did not let her words or looks affect me. I am not preoccupied with trying to be in another social group than what I am. God has placed me in this community and in my family for a reason, and I am content with that."

"Thank you."

They walked in silence for another moment or two, Jenny holding Emily's hand while Peter kept stride with them, his head lowered in deep reflection. Jenny glanced at him out of the corner of her eye and noticed his preoccupied manner. Hoping to draw him out of it, she attempted to strike up a conversation. "But Peter, I didn't realize your sister came from such a high part of society, or you, for that matter."

Peter sighed and scratched his chin, a habit he had formed years ago whenever he was preparing to discuss a subject he was not entirely comfortable with. "Yeah...I didn't think it mattered that much."

"You had just told us that you came from a wealthier family, but that you were trying to strike out for yourself. When you shared that, I never suspected that you meant you grew up on a plantation."

"I know, and I ask your forgiveness for that. I did not want people to judge me for my past, and so I downplayed it as much as I could without actually lying."

"But why did you not want people to know? We would not have judged you for growing up on a Virginia plantation."

Peter bit his lower lip, pausing before beginning his explanation. With a deep, slow breath, he began. "I am sorry for not being forthright with you or your family, and I ask your forgiveness for that. About a month ago, I spoke with your parents, James, and William and told them about how I truly was raised and where I am from. I felt I owed that much to your parents after everything they have done for me, and to your brothers, considering how close we have grown. And then after what happened today, I feel obliged to give you the same explanation.

"I grew up in some of the highest society in Virginia. My father has many friends in the government, and we were all the time taking trips to the Capital, attending balls anywhere within a reasonable driving distance, and supervising the production of tobacco and cotton. My family owns over three hundred slaves—at least, they did when I left two years ago. I did not think anything of the practice of slavery at all growing up. To me and Olivia, it was as natural for a Negro to be a slave as the sun coming up in the morning; it was a part of life.

"But then, when I was about seventeen, I was in the city with some of my upper class acquaintances, and as we were strolling through the streets, we came across a meeting in one of the churches. One of the boys acting as a crier told us that the minister was going to discuss the issue of equality among all members of society. We didn't have anything else to do, and it sounded interesting enough, so we agreed to attend the service. What began as something purely to while away an hour or two, turned into a moment that opened my eyes to a truth I had never seen before.

"The minister—I forget his name—was teaching how all men are on the same standing before God, male and female, slave and free. We all needed the Savior, no matter where we were in life. I already knew that, as did nearly everyone else in attendance. But then he showed that since everyone who was saved was only redeemed by the grace of God, no man had any room for boasting about his status. The minister explained, basing his arguments on passages from Scripture, that no man had any right to own another man. It was not living in the footsteps of Christ for an individual to use slave labor—even if he didn't treat them harshly.

"It was something I had never considered before that moment, something I had never even heard explained. But the Lord used that to begin convicting me about the institution of Slavery. I began to consider, reflecting on the passages the minister spoke out of, that it was wrong for me and my family to own all these slaves. After months of wrestling with the issue, I approached my Father with my concerns. He laughed at my childishness, explaining that I had gotten caught up in an emotional appeal. He argued that if we did not provide for the Negros, they could not survive on their own in America. Therefore, he reasoned, our family was doing them a favor in providing for their physical needs in exchange for labor. We continued to debate the subject for a substantial time, and it finally ended with him telling me that I would have to choose one or the other: either I would be an active member of the family as a plantation owner, or I would have to renounce all claims to the family's property.

"I imagine you can draw your own conclusions about what happened, but I left the house when I was eighteen, choosing the latter path of the two offered me. I could not reconcile the things I had seen in the Scriptures with my family's plantation, and so I could not remain there any longer. I have not severed all ties with my family, however. I still write and receive letters from my mother and sister, and Olivia has come and visited me a few times since I left. My father has not forbidden me to return, nor has he stopped talking with me, but he has made it quite plain in no uncertain terms that I can expect nothing from him in regards to monetary support or future inheritance.

"But I cannot in good conscience go back on what I have been convicted about. I know in my heart that the Bible teaches that slavery as we know it in America is wrong. I cannot deny what the Lord has shown me, and so I have not gone back. But the Lord has been so faithful to me. He has provided for my needs and blessed me in so many ways. I firmly believe that He will continue to provide in the future as I seek to follow Him and His word."

While Peter had been recounting the journey that had brought him to Chesson, he had kept his eyes straight ahead of him, a shadow seeming to creep over his face as he remembered those days of struggle with his conscience and the truth. But as he reached the turning point of the story, his face slowly began to lose the darkness, just as the wee morning hours slowly begin to rid themselves of the dark blanket that enveloped the earth, making room for the first golden rays to burst from behind the Blue Ridge Mountains. The effect was not lost on his companion as she walked by his side with her sister beside her. She had grown to look up to Peter like she did to William or James, and even her eldest brother John. Peter was always so reserved, especially around her, but each time he opened up, she found her admiration vindicated.

The three lapsed into silence at the close of his short tale. What could be said at a time like that? Peter, reserved as it was, did not feel like continuing the conversation, nor did he settle on another suitable topic. Jenny was unsure of how to respond to such a story, having never experienced anything worthy of comparison. And Emily was simply content to walk and admire the fleeting butterflies and scurrying ants they passed as she walked gripping her sister's hand. But they were almost at the Taylor home, so the silence did not continue long.

Arriving at the gate to their yard, Peter lifted the latch and swung the door open, motioning for the girls to proceed him. "This is where I leave you ladies," he informed his companions as they turned about.

Jenny protested, "Oh, but we have plenty of food. I am sure my parents would be delighted to have you join us for supper."

"I did not intend to stay, so please do not think that is why I accompanied you back."

"Not at all."

"Oh please, Peter," Emily added her plea to that of her sister's, smiling up at the young man.

Peter started to protest, but as he considered what he had awaiting him back at his own cabin, he felt his original intention being overruled by the offer of his generous neighbors. There was nothing at his own place that demanded his immediate return, and an evening in the company of friends would do him good.

Stepping through the gate, Peter acquiesced, "I suppose I could stay for supper."

As the trio continued their path towards the cabin, Peter's eye began to admire the quaint home and its surroundings. He always enjoyed simple scenes such as the one ahead of him, a cabin surrounded by acres of fields, especially when those fields were covered in a rich growth of wheat or corn. And though the fields laid bare on that winter day, the effect was only slightly diminished on Peter.

Turning his attention back towards the cabin, his eye landed upon the clothes line to the south side of the house. A quilt hung upon the line, waving gently in the breeze. Since his move to Chesson, Peter had begun to appreciate the rich heritage and stories often worked into the patterns of the quilts, but the Taylors possessed several that Peter had never seen anywhere else, and one of those hung upon the line then as they walked towards the house.

Commenting off-handedly, Peter gestured towards the quilt and said, "It seems that nearly every time I come by, you all have a quilt out on the line. I think they are beautiful, but I do admit, it does seem that it is an awfully large amount of quilts for just one family."

Jenny's eye shot between Peter and the quilt, then back again, her concern becoming apparent in the lines which creased her forehead for a brief instant. Trying to dispel any apprehension in her voice, she replied, "Oh, we don't really have that many. Ma likes us to air them out as often as we can, so it may seem that we have more than we actually do."

"I see. Though I have never been able to fully understand all of them, I have heard that quilts often tell stories of the families or of some past event."

"Many do, but some are just simple patterns of material that we cannot use for anything else."

"I understand. This quilt is one that I have often seen hanging when I come, and though I have tried to study it, I cannot seem to make much sense of the pattern. Do you know the story behind it?"

"Well, not exactly," Jenny tried to assume a nonchalant air. "I think it comes from a pattern that a friend of the family gave us some time ago. It is one that we have had for quite a while now, but I do not know everything about it."

Their steps had brought them to the cabin, and Peter opened the door for his companions. "Oh well, that is fine," he smiled. "I do not know what your mother has made for supper, but it smells wonderful."

CHAPTER FOUR

At the sound of a horse being reined to a halt immediately outside, Peter raised his eyes from the knob he had been attaching to a cabinet door and glanced towards the shop's front window, then turned to his employer. His questioning gaze found Samuel, who, wiping his hands on his well-worn leather apron, was already stepping to the door with a broad smile upon his face. Following a quick knock, the door to the shop swung inward on its hinges, revealing the frame of a young man still wrapped in a great coat, a hat pulled tightly upon his head. The youth was a few years older than Peter, but the neglect of his chin only produced a scraggly moss that gave him the appearance of a boy much younger than he actually was.

"My boy, come in," Samuel greeted heartily.

"Thank you, Grandfather," the young man replied brightly, taking Samuel's offered hand with eagerness. "It is so good to see you once again."

"As it is you, Nathan." Samuel closed the door from the biting wind of the November air. Turning around to face the shop's interior, he motioned towards the previously unacknowledged Peter. "You remember my apprentice, Peter Brenton?"

"Peter, of course. How are you these days?" Nathan cried and stretched out a calloused hand in greeting.

Peter returned the firm grip. "Quite well, Nathan. And how are you? I trust the weather was cooperative enough for your journey?"

"As well as could be expected," Nathan laughed. "I tell you, some nights out on the roads can be brutal with the way the wind manages to find a way through all of your clothes, no matter how near you draw up to a fire."

"Well, come warm yourself. Here, let me take your hat and coat," Samuel offered, gesturing towards the small, wood stove in the far corner of the shop, placed well away from the benches under which mounds of wood shavings had collected.

"Thank you, sir," Nathan replied, taking advantage of both of his grandfather's offers. He stepped to the stove and rubbed his hands together, allowing the warmth from the fire to wash over them. Hanging his arms by his side, Nathan turned around and surveyed the cabinet shop. "Well, by the looks of things, I would say business seems to be coming in pretty steadily. Are there more orders than usual this time of year?"

"More or less, it's about the same," Samuel shrugged nonchalantly. "Work comes in spurts, and this is usually the last big one until spring comes. In the winter months, people are less inclined to be spending their hard earned cash on something that would not be deemed a necessity."

Nathan nodded thoughtfully. "I can understand that. I've done a little carpentry work before, but I haven't occupied myself in the business for a long enough amount of time to gain an appreciation for the changing tides of orders."

"To be perfectly honest with you, I am surprised that we have had as much call for work as we have had, considering the tensions in our country right now."

As soon as Samuel had broached the subject of the conflict between the Northern and Southern states, it seemed as if a dark cloud fell upon the countenances of all three men in the small shop. The matter of states' rights in conjunction with the issues encompassing the institution of slavery was a topic fraught with tensions, even among friends, and as the temperatures had grown colder as the year turned from autumn to early winter, the conflict between the opposite sides of the strife grew increasingly heated.

Nathan nodded slowly, stuck his hands into his pockets, and strode to the bench where Samuel was carving a design onto a cabinet door. With solemnity in his voice, he concurred, "These times are rising with tension, and I am surprised that something has not yet happened, one way or the other."

"What do you mean by that?" Peter quarried, curiosity furrowing his brow.

With a glow of passion flickering in his young eye, Nathan turned to face him. "I hint at either a declaration declaring all men free, or the creation of a new country by the states south of the Mason-Dixon line." He returned his attention towards his grandfather. "Down in the Carolinas, this debate is rapidly spiraling into something that threatens to be much bloodier than anyone imagines."

Samuel raised his head, his grey eyes probing the young man deeply. "So you believe my fears of war are well founded?"

"If certain people have their way, I do not consider it an outlandish possibility. It might well be more real than most of us would care to admit. I would hate to think that these issues being wrestled with in our government would lead to brothers and fathers drawing each other's blood, and I pray to God that it will not come to that, yet it is a future that we must consider."

"I have long been concerned with that possibility," Samuel conceded, then continued in a lower voice, "in more ways than you may know."

Silence again reigned in the woodshop, each individual lapsing into contemplations within their own respective minds. Peter knew that all three of them present that day despised the practice of slavery in their nation, and that Samuel Kouffers reflected his grandson's aversion to anything close to war, yet still an uncomfortable spirit lay heavy upon him. Issues of controversy such as the ones that had been laid upon the table by Nathan were ones Peter made a habit of avoiding if at all practical, regardless of whether he personally agreed with the principle speaker or not.

Attempting a lighter tone, Peter interposed, "So Nathan, you mentioned that you had tried your hand at

The Choice

carpentry in the past—what kind of work do you find yourself occupied in now?"

"I've tried a few different things, but I believe I have finally settled upon surveying," Nathan shared, appreciating Peter's attempt to reverse the heaviness that had settled upon them all.

"Surveying?" Samuel repeated. "What led you to that?"

"Several things. Ma has a cousin who has been occupied in that line of work for many years now, and I began to help him out some a while back when work was beginning to slow at the mill in our town. I would lend a hand for a few weeks here and there, but I quickly came to love the job. I get to travel around some, see new places and all that. But I also am able to spend most days by myself out in the woods, or in a field of cotton or wheat all alone. The slaves are there, of course," the former darkness began to show itself again in his face, but he shook it off with a smile. "I mean, alone in terms of someone else actually working with me."

Peter's quick eye had caught the shadow that had threatened to creep across the other man's face, appreciating its significance. It affirmed his previous evaluation of Nathan's character and of his true opinion of slavery.

"I understand your enjoyment of being out in the open air," Peter sighed from his work and checked the alignment of the cabinet doors as they closed against each other. "There are many afternoons after I finished here with work that I will roam through these hills alone. I find it so refreshing. On most of those occasions, I will bring my Bible along with me and spend time at this one particular point in quiet meditation."

As Peter had been narrating his pleasurable afternoons, Nathan stole a sidelong glance at Samuel who gave an almost imperceptible nod of the head. As he finished, Nathan leaned against the post he had previously stood beside, affecting a casual manner. "That does sound like a good way to pass an afternoon. I'm afraid I appreciate more the opportunity to think and plan by myself without any interruptions from anyone else. That place you mentioned sounds like a dandy of a spot. I wouldn't mind seeing that before I leave, if you do not mind showing me, that is."

"Not in the least. I would be more than glad to show you."

"I will look forward to it. Do you all typically work on Saturdays?"

"Not unless we have a rush order," Samuel reported. "I was not planning on opening the shop in the morning, but Peter here sometimes comes by to pick up a tool or something."

"But that is not very often," Peter returned. "If you are not occupied with anything in particular tomorrow, you are welcome to come over if you would like."

"I would enjoy that very much," Nathan returned with a warm smile, a look in his eye that Peter could not exactly identify the meaning of.

The three men continued to converse throughout the afternoon, Samuel and Peter continuing their own work and Nathan lending a hand where he could be of use. The controversial matters that had been discussed were not raised again, but the conversations centered on exchanging news from the two respective regions of the country represented in the shop that afternoon.

As the sun began sinking lower in the western sky, Peter donned his own coat, giving directions to Nathan of how to find his cabin from the Kouffers' place. Nathan listened intently, repeated the distinctive points along the path that he would keep an alert eye for. With a final firm hand shake, Peter mounted his horse and began his journey home.

Nathan closed the door to the shop and turned to face his grandfather who waited expectantly. A knowing look in his eye, Samuel quarried, "Are you still certain he is the one you want to use for your plan?"

Nathan smiled. "Yes sir, he will be perfect for it."

■■

Peter laid a hand admiringly against the trunk of a towering oak above the Chesson Valley, turning to face

Nathan just a few paces behind him. For some unknown reason, the trees on the slope directly below their position did not send their spires as high as some of the surrounding vegetation, nor were they quite as dense, allowing a spectacular view of the valley below. It was one of Peter's favorite places to steal away to and simply rest in solitude, away from the cabin, away from his neighbors, away from everything—except God.

"This is the reason I come up here," Peter smiled, gesturing to the magnificent view that lay before them.

Nathan followed Peter's indication, his eyes filling with awe as he beheld the scene spread out before his eyes. "You were right," he conceded. "This is well worth the journey up these slopes."

"It is simply breathtaking in the fall," Peter commented, his eyes taking on a far-off look as he reflected on the memory of the spectacular display of vibrant colors of the changing tones of the foliage. "It is so peaceful to come up here and simply rest in this beauty. I have often made the climb when I have had difficult decisions to make, and I have found the answers I have been seeking for as I spend time in reflection and in prayer."

He pulled himself from his reverie and faced his friend. "Is there a place like this near your home where you often steal away to think in moments of silence?"

Nathan slowly shook his head, still admiring the valley below. "No," he began slowly, "I'm afraid not. But then again, I have never been the type of man who prefers to spend more time than necessary in considering a matter before I act." He turned back towards Peter. "I know that may sound strange or even reckless, but once I make up my mind, I do not waste any more time before I carry out my plan."

Peter nodded, though more in acknowledgement than understanding. "My friend William is like that. More often than not, he gets swept up in the fervor of his older brother. He will hear both sides of an issue, make up his mind, and proceed with his decision, yet I fear without as much evaluation as he should have devoted to it."

Nathan chuckled inwardly at Peter's reflections. He knew that Peter was more given to slow, methodical contemplations, yet it still sounded odd to hear him actually voice it. "If you had seen me with some choices I have made, you would probably pass the same judgement upon me. But—" he suddenly grew solemn, studying Peter intently. "There is a decision I want to present to you, a plan that I have been a part of for some time now."

An uneasy sensation crept over Peter. He had heard James, and even Seth Mason, speak of pockets of rebellion growing throughout the South. He thought he knew Nathan enough to excuse him from such activity, but what else could he mean by what he had said? Still, Peter tried to quiet his apprehension, he did not know what Nathan actually intended to set before him.

"A plan? I'm sorry, but—"

"Not here," Nathan emphatically shook his head. "I would be able to speak more freely and explain my meaning more clearly if we were actually back at your cabin. It is a matter of great, the greatest importance."

With dread continuing to settle upon Peter, he descended the side of the mountain, Nathan following close behind him. The words Nathan had chosen were ones he had heard Seth use in conjunction with an uprising just a few days previously, only confirming his already wary attitude towards Nathan's manner.

As the pair approached the cabin, from which a thin billow of grey smoke speckled with black ash rolled, Nathan commented off-handedly, "On my way over this morning, it seemed to me that your cabin sits a little secluded from the main road. If it hadn't been for that Hickory with that burl on the side of it, I might have easily missed the cabin."

"It is set back from the road some, but I do not mind it. I like being alone, left to myself, and this place affords me that."

"So I take it you do not get many visitors," Nathan prodded, studying his companion closely.

"No," Peter replied guardedly, unsure of why that particular fact of information mattered to the young man. "Not usually. But then again, I live by myself, and I don't have much to offer anyone, so there is hardly a reason for anyone to call."

"I understand." Nathan lapsed into silence, his eyes searching the surrounding landscape as if searching for something. His manner disconcerted Peter. Ever since he had arrived after dinner, something had seemed slightly different about Nathan, almost as if the man had an air of secrecy about him.

Proceeding his companion, Peter stepped onto the porch and opened the door, motioning him inside. Nathan entered, laying his hat on the rack immediately inside the room, admiring the cabin's interior with an easy air. "This is a fine place you have here, Peter."

"Thank you, but I'm afraid it's not much." He had a small table surrounded by a few chairs he had carved himself, a small cot in one corner covered with a few sheets that he could never perfect the art of folding, and a small bread cabinet in which he kept small quantities of flour, meal, and other such supplies. A fireplace lay in the middle of one of the longest walls of the cabin, a simple stone mantle surrounding it, his Springfield rifle resting on its hooks above, which Nathan stood admiring.

"I've had that rifle a few years now," Peter explained, closing the door behind him and moving to Nathan's side. "I purchased it shortly before I moved here last summer."

"It is a beauty of a gun," Nathan commented. "I have a Springfield myself, but it's several years older than this one." He pulled his eyes away from the gun and surveyed the room once again, finally resting on the small door cut into the wall beside Peter's cot. "Where does that door lead?"

"It just leads out back," Peter responded slowly, his brow creasing even more with concern and bewilderment at his friend's intense curiosity about his person and cabin. "A root cellar lies about a hundred paces behind it, so I suppose it was built as a quicker way to access that."

Nathan nodded, stroking his stubble-covered chin thoughtfully. "I see, I see..." As if making a sudden decision himself, he spun around with determination etched in his young face. It was not a look of aggression, yet this sudden reversal fanned Peter's abundant apprehension.

"Peter," Nathan began, "please, take a seat."

Peter complied as Nathan moved towards the fireplace and rested his arm upon the mantle. Staring into the fire, but seeing something else in his mind, Nathan continued, "Peter, there has been something I have wanted to discuss with you for some time now, something that could change the lives for many people, people who deserve that change. I have been involved in this work for some time now. Surveying just allowed me to engage in it more fully," he smiled into the fire. "I have seen this need all my life, but especially over the past five or seven years. I see a people condemned to carry a burden that was never theirs to bare, a weight unjustly placed upon them with seemingly no way for it to be removed.

"Yet there are those of us who feel that things can change, that they do not have to stay the same. We are not many, some you might not even guess if you would see them in the street. But we are there, all throughout this country—and we are growing, Peter. We need more men, women—young men, young women to fill our ranks. We need men who will be willing to give their lives to help us," he raised his head to meet Peter's gaze, "and I believe you would want to be one of those men."

"Nathan, I, uh," Peter coughed, groping for words, "I appreciate you sharing this with me, but I cannot condone or engage in any such activities."

Nathan's brow furrowed, his head tilting to one side. "What do you mean? I thought you would be eager to join us, to devote your life to this cause."

"I cannot join you because I feel that, at our current political situation, it would go against the Word of God."

Now Nathan stood confounded, entirely bewildered by Peter's response. "Against the...how can freedom from evil oppression be against the Bible?"

"But it's not evil—"

"No," Nathan shouted, straightening with fire blazing in his own eyes, and not from any reflection of the flames dancing upon the logs near his feet. "No, Peter. Slavery is wrong in any form, and especially the way we conduct it here in America!"

"Slave...slavery?" Peter repeated the word, as if unable to comprehend its meaning.

"Yes, slavery," Nathan returned, perplexed by the young man's seeming incomprehension of his offer. "What did you think I was meaning?"

Pulling himself from his reflective attitude, Peter explained, "Forgive me, I took your offer wrong. For a while there, you had me thinking you meant forming a Confederacy."

A light of understanding dawned in Nathan's eyes as he realized the source of their misunderstanding. "Confederacy? Hah!" He spat into the fire. "Confederacy. Let Davis and Clay argue for that in Congress. You know that I have no desire to support and or advocate such a proposition."

"That is what I had thought, based upon our previous conversations and the letters you sent your grandfather. So, when you start talking about delivering from unjust oppression, it seemed so out of character for you. But if you didn't mean forming a Southern nation, what do you mean?"

"You ever hear tell of the Underground Railroad?"

"No, don't believe I have. That would be something to see, I admit, but how could that pertain to anything about bringing freedom to slaves?"

"Let me tell you. It's not what you may be thinking." Nathan pulled up a chair across from Peter and proceeded to explain about the hidden network of individuals who all cooperated to provide paths for slaves to escape to freedom in the North. Some of them helped guide the runaways by night to safe houses, which he explained were called stations, where they would be hidden during the day until they resumed their flight again as darkness fell. There were stations all across the South, but they kept needing to find more, since the slave catchers kept finding some of them.

"Now I will warn you, it is a dangerous business," Nathan admitted, drawing his description to a close. "When the slaves come to a safe house, the head of the family is promising to protect them with his life. The slave catchers will stop at nothing to recapture a runaway, especially if he was considered valuable by his former master and a price has been set on his head. The same danger falls upon the conductors. I know this is a lot to ask, but if I and my grandfather have been an accurate judge of character, I believe you would fill the position we are looking for with excellence."

Words formed slowly in Peter's mind, his thoughts swirling about as he tried to sort through the deluge of information Nathan had just revealed. He had heard rumors of just such a secret network to help slaves escape, but he had heard such varied reports that he was uncertain of any of their validity. Yet he could not deny that proof of the existence of the network was sitting in a chair in his cabin right in front of him.

"You, uh," Peter coughed, "you said Mr. Kouffers knew about this? Was he aware of what you are doing, and that you are asking me to join you?"

"In a way, yes. I have only recently told him of my work in the Underground, though I am sure he has had his suspicions for some time now. I told him of my plan to recruit someone in this area to our work, and he heartily consented to my asking you."

"Our work? If your grandfather knows about and supports the Underground, why does he not turn his house into a station? I am not trying to force anything onto him that I would not accept myself, but I do not see how I can provide what you are asking. I live by myself, I work the entire day for most of the week at the cabinet shop, and I have no place to hide anyone. If your grandfather is so supportive, would he not be a better option?"

Nathan cocked his head to one side in perplexity. "My grandfather would help I know if I asked him, but it is not a station master that I am looking for."

"Isn't that what you are asking? You have told me about a network that helps slaves escape, providing safe shelter for them to stay during the day—is not that what you need?"

"No. What I am looking for is a conductor, someone to help guide the slaves along the paths they need to take. When they leave the plantations, they know little more than that they must run north and that friends await them along the way. We need men who will be willing to be their guides.

"You would still work here for my grandfather, of course, yet only not as much. If you accepted, it would mean making runs on a regular basis. I would be able to have the information you would need ready at the proper time, such as where to go and things."

"Wha, what do you mean by runs?"

"I mean trips further south, then up into Pennsylvania."

"All that way? Nathan, do you know how long that would take?"

Nodding his head, he conceded, "I do. I have made the trip several times myself. Conductors are needed, Peter. We need you."

"But what about my absence here in the community—"

Nathan raised his hand. "Hold on, hold on. I know you need time to think this through. I am not asking for a decision right now. What I am asking, however, is that you consider this as a work you could be involved in to help bring freedom to so many. We cannot sit around waiting for something to happen 'one day.' If things are going to change, they have to change now...and we are the ones who will bring it about."

CHAPTER FIVE

Shaking his head in an attempt to clear his mind, Peter glanced down at the sketched-out design of a cupboard Samuel had given him to build. Try as he might, he could not keep his attention fixed upon his task at hand. Not then, not after what they had discovered the previous day.

It had finally happened, the rip had started. A few days past, South Carolina had severed all ties with the government in Washington, declaring secession from the Union. The news was met with a mixture of elation and sorrow in Chesson, as it was in the rest of the country. Elation in the hearts of those desiring a Southern nation, but sorrow on the part of those who glimpsed the darkness that lay in the future.

As soon as they had received word of his state's decision, Nathan prepared to return to his home, cutting his stay with the Kouffers short by several days. Peter knew his friend had no other choice, but still he desired that he could have stayed longer. He still had so many questions, questions that needed answers…

Shaking himself once again, Peter reached for the wooden ruler laying on the bench top to his left. He would have to sort through his dilemma later; he had to get this cabinet finished. Chesson was part of Virginia, not South Carolina. Life had to go on, regardless of the weight settling in his heart.

As he strode to the stack of lumber on the far side of the shop, Peter slowed as he surveyed the different species of wood set upon the racks. Turning round to face Samuel, he inquired, "Mr. Kouffers, are we all out of cherry?"

His employer glanced up from the board upon which he had been shaping a profile with a hand plane. "I reckon so, but Hill said he would be bringing another load by here in a couple of days. What were you needing it fer?"

"That job for the Chambers. I was about to commence upon the cupboard for that set."

"Oh, I remember," he nodded. "I put cherry down on that cabinet, since that was the sample they had looked at, but they were not particular that it had to be made of that wood. When we had talked, they told me to use whatever wood we had at hand. So, I would go ahead and use some of that alder, since it has a similar color and there is a large set of clear boards laid up over yonder on that bottom rack."

"Yes sir." Peter turned and selected a board of a proper width for the project he was occupied with.

"Is there something on your mind, Peter?"

Laying the board upon his work table, Peter queried, "Sir?"

"You seem a little distracted, as if your mind is somewheres else. Is it this matter down in the Carolinas?"

"It is," Peter sighed. "I have been praying that it would not come to this point, yet it has."

"There are many of us that have been praying that way," Samuel made a final stroke with the hand plane. "And yet as you said, it has come to this point, and I fear this is only the beginning."

"What do you mean?"

"What I mean is that this will not end with only South Carolina. She has set this country aflame, and I tremble to think of how far it will spread."

"How far it will spread?"

"It is only a matter of time," Samuel sighed. Gesturing towards the stove beyond Peter, he continued, "Those flames in that fire place are slowly consuming the logs, reducing them to a mere pile of ashes to be scooped up and dumped in a waste heap. And that is what is happening to the Union. I know that tensions have been rising for years between the North and the South, but they are beginning to come to a head with South Carolina's secession. From the looks of things, Alabama, Mississippi, and the rest of the South won't be far behind her."

A far-off haze creeping into his eyes, Samuel laid his tool beside the board and leaned against his own table. "It's as if the two parts of our country are two mules hitched together as a team, trying to draw a cart with many precious valuables. One mule is the North, the other is the South, and the yoke tying them together is the Union. The cart is filled with every day, ordinary people of this nation. People such as you and me, the Taylors, my children and grandchildren. These two mules began snorting at one another, then commenced to nipping at the other's mane and ears. Now they have begun kickin' at each other. I tell you the truth, Peter, it will not take much more for the yoke to break—and much irreversible harm will come to the people of our great nation."

Silence fell upon the shop as Peter reflected upon the older man's words. Though he did not wish to admit it, he knew Samuel's estimation was correct. War was coming, and they could not escape. Even if Virginia stayed in the Union, they would be called upon for volunteers to help put down the rebellion. Either way, the conflict would come upon them.

The thought angered Peter. There he was, trying to live a quiet life in all godliness and honesty, just as Paul had commanded Timothy in scripture, yet he was being drawn into something he had taken no part in. *And why now? Every time I am about to reach a decision, why does something happen that prevents me from following that choice?* He glanced down at the board laying in front of him, unsure of how to answer either his employer or the questions in his own swirling mind.

Taking up his tool once again, Samuel resumed his work. "Forgive me, I did not mean to make speeches."

"No sir, that is fine," Peter returned slowly, contemplatively. "It gives me much to think about. I have not heard it expressed quite that way before, but what you have said seems to be the logical result of what is happening right now in our country."

"I pray that by some miracle it will not be, but if reconciliation is not reached..." He wagged his head, forcing a low chuckle. "There I go again, making speeches. Once I finish these panels here, I will come take a look at making them doors for that set, hear?"

"Yes sir."

What remained of the afternoon passed as nearly every other day Peter had worked in the shop, but his mind spun with his silent contemplations. He could not shake Samuel's words, or the issues that they represented. With secession having become a reality and the threat of more states leaving the Union looming before them, he felt himself at a loss to know how to answer Nathan's proposal.

As he walked the few miles to his cabin, Peter wondered if the bleakness of winter that gripped their valley was symbolic of what awaited their nation. Judging from their earlier conversation, he knew Samuel believed it did. Maybe, he tried to persuade himself, maybe he was being over cautious. Yet even as the thought formed within him, Peter knew it was only wishful thinking to turn a blind eye to the trouble brewing, foolish to not consider what lay before them.

"Afternoon, Peter."

He started, and as he searched for the voice, he found Henry trotting up the lane towards him. He had come all the way to the Taylors without realizing it.

"Hello. How are you?" he inquired of his young neighbor.

"Fine, thank ya. Ma said we's got a whole mess of meat and taters on for supper, and she was a askin' me to see if you'd come eat with us tonight. Will ya?"

Peter slowly shook his head. "I'm afraid I will not be able to make it."

"How come?" the boy inquired, his eyebrows knitting together in curiosity.

"I need...uh, you see...I have a few things to attend to back at my place."

The ambiguous response offered was insufficient for the young neighbor; it only served to whet his curiosity. He scampered alongside Peter for several hundred yards, pelting him with questions as if they were little pebbles that could pierce the young man's armor of inner withdraw, but his queries were offered in vain; Peter would not divulge anything more than he had already told the boy.

Seeing that continuing his barrage of questions would be a fruitless effort, Henry wished Peter a good evening and returned to his family's farm dejectedly. The boy's manner only added to Peter's struggle. How he wished that the issues surrounding his country would resolve themselves that night and he could share the simple attitude of his young friend. Many an afternoon Peter had seen the boy frolicking across the Virginia hills, lost in a world of his own, completely oblivious to the threat of war which many believed loomed along the horizon like a thick cloud in mid-June.

Once inside his own cabin, Peter poured himself a generous mug of coffee and sank into one of the chairs by the fireplace. Sipping the steaming liquid, he stared absently into the fire, the dancing flames mimicking the shifting and twisting of the thoughts inside his mind.

He had not told Samuel of Nathan's request, nor had the older craftsmen brought the subject up in any of their conversations over the past several days. With Nathan having left the valley, Peter was left to consider his options alone. Nathan had said before he left, however, that Peter should write to him about his decision with the "surveying position" if he chose to accept. The young man had revealed nothing about the identity of other conductors or even of local station masters, and Peter could only guess who they might be, if they were even there in Chesson.

As he had considered the proposition, Peter felt himself torn from two directions. He earnestly desired to help bring freedom to the slaves, yet he did not see how he could be a conductor in the underground work. He lived by himself and he had no one to tend to his small farm while he was away. He depended entirely on his own labor for his substance, but if he assumed the role offered him, his time to engage in earning money or growing his food would be vastly limited.

He tried to argue with himself, to point out that the Lord would provide for his needs. However, another objection had risen in his mind as he tried to reconcile respect for the government with this seemingly illegal activity. Slaves were recognized by their nation as property, even though they were men and women, flesh and blood. Even though he abhorred the institution, if he helped them escape to freedom by leading them away from the plantations, was it not something akin to thievery? Furthermore, his conscience also argued with him, bickering about the possibility of having to lie to conceal run-aways. He was not actually hiding them, but he knew where they would be and would be assisting them in their flight. He did not know if he could do that.

Yet if his situation was not complicated enough, the threat of more states seceding added weight to both options he faced. On the one hand, if he was helping slaves escape from states that had formed another nation, he would not be resisting his own government by that work. But on the other, if he accepted on the sole basis of that prospect, he was founding his choice on a circumstance that might or might not come about. He did not know how many states would secede, or even if they would be successful in creating their own nation.

He sighed, taking another drink from his mug. He simply did not know how to choose. He placed the cup upon the floor at his feet, then knelt in prayer, pouring out his heart to his Heavenly Father, begging for wisdom and guidance in the decision he now faced.

With a grunt of exertion, Peter brought the ax crashing into the root of the oak stump. The old tree had broken off a few feet above the ground when a bolt of lightning struck it the previous summer during a thunderstorm, and though it lay towards the edge of one of their fields, the Taylors had not pulled the stump out. It was quite large, requiring a substantial amount of time to remove, and they had left it until the less-filled months of winter allowed them time to grapple with the task.

That January afternoon, being a little short on work at the cabinet shop, Peter occupied himself as he often did in helping his neighbors. He had noted the stump's position in the field, and when Charles had remarked that they had not had time to deal with it yet, he offered to remove it himself it they would like. Charles had heartedly consented, and Henry had volunteered to go along and keep Peter company, lending a hand as he could. Though not sure how much assistance the boy could be, Peter enjoyed his company and accepted his offer.

With another stroke of the ax, the remaining sinews of the root splintered and the blade broke free into the earth beneath. Peter paused to wipe the sweat from his brow. "Alright, Henry, that's the last one." He climbed out of the hole he had dug around the stump and laid the tool upon the ground.

"What do ya want me doing now?" Henry queried, eager to be of any assistance to his friend.

"Come on and bring Ole June and Dave over here now, if you will, and we'll get them hitched up."

Henry led the pair of horses and Peter positioned them facing away from the stump, leaving the old wagon tongue they drug between them and the root ball. After securing the chain they had brought between the yoke and the trunk of the tree, Peter took up a long metal bar and drove it into the ground under one of the largest roots. "Alright now, get them moving, but stay clear, hear?"

"Get up, girl! Come on, June," Henry coaxed as he pulled upon the reins of the mare to urge her to start. Snorting as they flung their heads, the horses leaned into their harness and strained forward, drawing the chain tight against the stump.

"That's it, get on up, Dave!" Peter hollered as he pulled down on the lever he had wedged under the stump, clicking his tongue at the horses.

Beginning to yield under the combined strain of the chain and the pressure from the metal bar, the stump started to lean forward, lifting itself out of the ground. Peter drove his wedge in afresh and pulled down with fresh vigor. "That's it now, come on."

A splintering noise arrested Peter's attention and he jerked his head up, surveying the scene. It had not come from the stump. "Henry, you hear something?"

"Sounds like it's a breakin' up to me," he called in reply.

"No, I don't think—" the sound came again, accompanied this time by the stump settling back into the hole it was partially pulled from. Peter drove the bar in deeper then leapt out of the depression he stood in. "Whoa, June! Dave, hold on!" He raced around and grabbed the horses' halters, leading them gently backwards until the slack returned to the chain they drug. He surveyed the horses, looking for anything out of place. They did seem a little out of line with each other, he realized, but their harnesses wouldn't have made any sound like he had heard, and their yoke still seemed sound.

Stepping around behind them, Peter found the wooden tongue splintered nearly in two, forming a slight "V" shape with its point facing the stump. He could not work with a broken tongue, and the stump was too large for only one horse to drag out.

Henry stepped to his side. "What's the matter? Should I start them pulling again?"

Peter slowly shook his head and pointed to the broken tongue. "Naw, not yet. We cannot work with that."

"Well, couldn't ya fix it?"

"I'm afraid not. It is made from a solid piece of wood, and it cannot be repaired, not with what I have available to use." He looked down at the boy. "Does your father have another one we could use out in the barn?"

"Naw, not that I remember. I think this was the only one we were not already usin'."

"What about an old yoke or something?"

Henry shook his head. "No, he doesn't keep those things lying 'round the barn."

Turning back to the stump, observing its stubborn position in the ground, he grimaced as he racked his mind to consider where he might find a replacement.

"Wait," Henry murmured slowly, "I think I heard Pa tellin' James one time that he kept old farm tools up in the old shed."

"Is that a fact? Well, come on; there might be one in there."

Henry did not move, standing still and gazing up at the young man.

"Something wrong, Henry?"

"Pa said I'm not to go up there. Says it is too dangerous."

Biting his lip, Peter considered the image in his mind of the old shed Henry referenced. He had never been inside the old cabin, nor all that close to it, but from his casual inspection, it seemed fairly sturdy. It certainly was not about to fall to pieces.

"I think it is safe enough," he mused.

"I don't know…Pa said I had to stay away and not play near it or anything."

"Tell you what," Peter nodded, "you stay here with the horses, and I will run up there and see what I can find."

Peter turned and started at a brisk pace for the field where he knew the outbuilding lay. It was not a far distance, but he did not wish to waste any more time than necessary in replacing the tongue. He could use almost anything: another solid beam with some rope, a discarded wagon axle, nearly anything could be used. Rounding a curve in the tree line, he surveyed the structure. It seemed in tolerable condition, but then again, maybe the rafters or interior posts were rotting. Striding up to the front of the shed, Peter pushed the door open upon its hinges and stepped into the darkness inside.

■■

"Henry," William called, drawing his own mare up as he approached his brother standing by the pair of horses near the old stump. "How is it going?"

Looking up at his brother, Henry replied, "It was going 'long fine, till the wagon tongue snapped, but we are gettin' it fixed."

"I knew it was getting old, but I thought it had strength in it yet," he commented, glancing towards the stump. "Yet then again, that is quite a load ya'll are trying to drag out of there."

"Ain't it? Peter said we 'bout got it, and it won't take much more to break it free."

William scanned the field and the nearby tree line. "Where is Peter at?"

"Aw, he's gone to find another yoke or wagon tongue so we can pull this out."

"I don't think Pa has another one up at the barn…" William's brow furrowed.

"I told him that, but he's heading up to the old cabin to look for one."

William's head snapped back towards his brother, drilling him with his eyes. "You mean that old shed up on that hill on the South side?"

'Yeah, I told him Pa said—"

"Hang it!" William muttered, whipping his horse into a full gallop, not waiting to hear the rest of the boy's explanation. He couldn't let Peter find what was in there.

■■

Peter blinked in the darkness, his eyes adjusting to the shed's interior. It seemed to be mostly empty, but a few barrels sat stacked to one side. Several shelves lined the back wall, separated in the middle by a low door. He found an assortment of farming implements and tool handles lying in one corner in a partially ordered fashion.

He stepped towards them, but a movement coming from the direction of the barrels caught his quick ear. Pausing in his stride, he listened intently. In the dim light, he narrowly eyed the corner as he approached, then as the barrel moved again, he stopped dead in his tracks.

■■

Kicking his horse for the last push to the shed, William raced up the low slope, his eyes searching. Peter could not be found, and that wasn't a good sign. As he neared the cabin, his heart sank even lower—the door was partially opened.

Reigning to a halt, William leapt from the saddle and raced for the door. To his dismay, he found Peter already inside staring at something he could not see, but he knew what it was. He had found them.

At William's entrance, Peter whipped his head towards his friend. "Will, how did…"

"We don't have any tongues up here, or any old wagon parts at all. I might find one at the mill. There's nothing in here."

"But—"

"Peter, please—we still have a lot to do today."

"Do you know about them?" Peter pointed towards the corner and William followed his gaze.

There in the corner behind the barrels stood four Negros: one man, two woman, one small boy. Their eyes contained mixtures of fear, worry, and concern, fear being the most prominent.

"Peter, you must not tell anyone what you have seen here—do you understand me?"

"But what are they doing out here? If they work for your family, why do they not live in the small homes like Shawna and Zirus?"

William sighed, "They don't because they do not work for us."

"Then who's…" Peter stopped as he realized the meaning behind William's words. His eyes found the cowering men and women, then returned to his friend. "They are runaways?"

"As I said, you must never speak of this to anyone."

"You are hiding runaways? Your family works for the Underground and this, this is a station?"

William stiffened, his eyes narrowing. "How did you know those terms?"

"So it is true then?"

"Who told you?"

"Nathan Lee Kouffers. He said there was a secret network that assisted runaways on their way to freedom, but he never said…"

William laid hold of his arm and turned to face the runaways. "You all stay here for now. I will return when it is dark. Peter will not tell anything, I give you my word." He faced his friend as he pulled him from the shed.

"I would never tell about this to anyone."

"I know, but I have to be sure," William sighed as he closed the door behind them. "No one must ever know. I will pick up another chain at the barn, and I believe we can get that stump out. But do not breathe a word of this to Henry. Not all of my family knows about this, so when I say no one, I mean exactly that: no one."

CHAPTER SIX

"…So, work's been slowing down for us. How 'bout you, Peter?" queried Charles Taylor. They had invited Peter to join them for dinner after services that Sunday afternoon, and he had heartily consented. Mary had prepared most of the meal—a roast along with some potatoes and green beans—and nearly every plate around the table was wiped clean. With Shawna, Mary, and Jenny, the Taylors could never be accused of eating 'bland' country cooking.

Peter had lapsed into one of his silent contemplations again, becoming oblivious to the conversations around him. Over the past three days, Peter had wrestled with his conscience about his discovery in the Taylor's old shed. The fact that they were a part of a secret network that he had not even known existed before two weeks ago bewildered him. But then, as he considered it more fully, he could not believe that they carried on their work without anyone being the wiser. They appeared as normal citizens, but a portion of their lives remained veiled from others in their community.

What troubled him was the matter of truthfulness in his relationship to the Taylors. It had taken him nearly fourteen months, but he had revealed his true past to them, being perfectly honest with his friends. And now that he had stumbled upon what he had, he felt obliged to tell Charles that he knew. He had only apologized for breaking the tongue while pulling out the stump, offering to purchase a new one to replace it. William had helped him drag the stump out with the additional horse and chain, and no one else knew of what had truly transpired that afternoon.

And William implored him to tell no one, not even other members of the family. *Surely William did not include his parents in that,* he reasoned to himself. *Of course they had to know about the work. Why else had Mr. Taylor warned Henry to stay away from the shed?* Yet still he wondered whether he should follow William's plea—command—or if he should reveal his new knowledge to Charles.

Peter shook himself to clear his mind, bringing himself to his present surroundings. Mentally chiding himself for his marked rudeness, he apologized, "I beg your pardon; I must have slipped into one of my moods. Can I ask you to repeat that, sir? I didn't quite make out the last part of your question."

Charles swallowed the potatoes he had been chewing, then repeated, "That's okay. I was only asking if you and Mr. Kouffers were running a little low on work still."

"A little, but we are starting to pick up some more work. I do have to remember, though, that it is January, so not very many people desire to start a large project this time of year."

"I would agree with that," William joined the conversation, setting his coffee cup back on the oaken table. "I know that if I can find something else to do during these few months, I will definitely avail myself of the opportunity without a second thought. And since there are no crops to harvest, there's not much to grind up at the mill—excusing what's been stored up since last fall."

"I can understand that," Peter conceded.

"Still," Charles leaned back in his chair. "Folks a'got to eat, so's I am glad that the Lord has seen fit to give us an adequate supply of grain. Both to give us work and to keep bread on the table."

James wiped his mouth on his shirt sleeve and received a correcting admonishing of the eyes from Jenny. Though she claimed that she didn't desire to be part of a higher level of society than she already was, Jenny did believe in using proper manners—something James never seemed to grasp. He winked teasingly at his younger sister, then turned to face Peter. "Hey, Pete, have you talked to Seth recently?"

Peter tried to restrain his feelings and not allow his opinion of the new subject to appear on his face. Seth was another one of the young men in Chesson that was a stanch Confederate—even more so with the recent political developments with South Carolina. Trying to sound civil, he remarked, "To be honest, no I have not. The Masons and I do not usually cross paths—besides meetin's—so I don't have much of an opportunity to speak with Seth."

"I understand. He was telling me this morning that he received a letter from his uncle down in Mississippi.

Apparently, they are planning to join South Carolina in secession soon, maybe as soon as this week. Seth was all worked up over it, and for good reason. Think of it—there might be two states in the Confederacy by this time next week!"

James' voice had been growing with excitement as he shared the news from further South, yet as he did so, a heavy cloud seemed to fall upon the other members gathered around the table. William dropped his eyes to his plate, moving his potato cubes around with his fork. Jenny began chewing her lower lip, conscious of how sore a subject secession was between James and her father. Charles' face darkened with concern—whether for his country or his son, Peter could not tell. And as for himself, Peter felt his thumbs instinctively start rubbing themselves against the fingers of their respective hands. James knew full well how the rest of his family felt about this topic, and Peter had hoped he would refrain from bringing it up on the Lord's Day.

With her voice filled with a motherly warning, Mary tried to quell the storm she feared was brewing. "James—"

"But Ma, it's true. I was talking with Jones just last week, and he was saying—"

"James!" All eyes immediately riveted themselves on Charles Taylor. He never raised his voice—especially at the table, and never with company. He had not actually yelled, but the volume and tone of his voice demanded attention. When he spoke again, he chose his words slowly and deliberately. "That will be enough.

You know that I have asked you to not bring up anything dealing with secession at this table on the day given to the Lord. Can't you see that this day is holy to our God? It is the day our Savior conquered the grave, and we are to honor it in all we do on this day. I do not want to hear anything else about the subject, do you understand me?"

Though fires of passion roared behind his eyes, James responded, "Yes, sir." The conversation was far from over in his mind, but he would not transgress his father's command, more so with Peter's presence at the table. Though the subject dropped from conversation, tension lingered around the table, shrouding the home like a thick fog, weighing heavy upon each spirit.

As Jenny rose with a forced smile, trying to dispel the gloom settling in her family's home, she announced, "Well, I do believe the apple pie is nearly ready. I'll go fetch it; it will be a fine way to finish off this delicious meal you made, Ma."

"Thank you, Jenny. One of your pies will round this off nicely," Mary attempted an easy manner, grateful for any diversion from the recent subject. Jenny's ability to keep peace amongst the family was something she thanked the Lord for daily. And their family needed it now more than ever.

As Jenny returned with the desired dessert, Peter drew the conversation back to the point before James' distasteful detour. "I had mentioned earlier about things being a little slower. Mr. Kouffers has been finding enough work for us to do most days, but I do have more time than I was accustomed to for my own work at my home."

"I'm glad you mentioned that," Charles' face began to soften as he turned his attention to his young neighbor sitting across the table from him. "That's been something me and Mary's been a'meaning to ask you. Our old dresser's 'bout worn all to pieces, and we were hoping you might be able to find the time to make us a new one."

"I would consider it an honor to build that for you and your wife, sir." Peter always leapt at the chance to hone his woodworking skills on the days he was not employed at Samuel's shop.

"Excellent," encouraged Charles. "It is something I have been putting off for quite a while, and you mentioning about having some extra time on your hands reminded me of it." Charles helped himself to a slice of his daughter's pie. "And speakin' of excellent, I am sure looking forward to this." The other members of the family began retrieving slices of the two pies set upon the table and commenced partaking of the warm dessert.

Later that afternoon, as he was taking his leave of his amiable neighbors, Charles joined Peter as the young man began moving to the door. "Allow me to walk out with you," he remarked softly.

"Thank you, sir. Good evening, everyone." The two men stepped outside, followed by a chorus of farewells, and the pair began strolling towards the gate of the yard.

Charles was the first to break the silence. "Peter, I want to apologize for my conduct this afternoon when James started talking about the rebellion brewing. It is becoming an increasingly contentious subject between me and my son, but I have no excuse for my response to his words. I ask your forgiveness."

"I forgive you, sir. But I understand your heart, and that you want to not bring up a subject that can cause so much worry on the Lord's Day."

"Thank you, Peter."

They continued walking for a moment, each remembering the afternoon's subject that had cast such a gloom over their meal. Stealing a furtive glance at his companion, Peter considered whether he should tell him about the shed. Charles had humbled himself by apologizing, going far beyond what was required. He did not have to walk out with him like he did, but he had chosen to because of his respect for the young man. How could he neglect or ignore that?

Hesitantly, Peter began, "Mr. Taylor?"

"What is it, son?"

"I forgot to ask you earlier, but I was thinking about that dresser you wish me to make."

"What's on your mind?"

"I can come up with a basic design on my own, but I would want you and Mrs. Taylor to look over them before I actually began building the cabinet."

"That will be fine."

"But I have a lot of the different wood I can use at my place, and so, if it's not too much of an imposition, I was wondering if I could ask you and your wife to come out and look at some different designs and wood I could use for it. And," he hesitated before continuing, "and there is something I wanted to discuss with you all, a matter that has been weighing on my heart and conscience."

Charles studied him with his eyes as if trying to discern more of the guarded revelation. With a simple nod of the head, he replied, "That will be no trouble at all. And I completely understand. I don't believe we have any plans for tomorrow afternoon—would that work for you?"

"Yes sir, that will be fine."

■■■

"Alright. The hickory will go quite well with this stain." Peter replaced the board he had just dabbed a stain on back upon the workbench in his barn. Not much time had elapsed after Peter returned from work before his neighbors Charles and Mary had arrived in their wagon. They had retreated to his barn to examine a few samples of wood type and stain color he had prepared, finally settling on the one he had just indicated.

"And in terms of the design," Charles directed the conversation. "Mary and I are satisfied with the style we have now. The only reason we are having this one made is that our old one is falling apart."

"That will be fine," Peter nodded. "When a practicable time is for you, I will come take down some measurements for it, and I will begin as soon as possible."

Peter and his guests turned and began retracing their steps towards the barn's open doors. "I want to thank you for coming this afternoon."

"You are welcome. Thank you for being willin' to build this for us." As they approached the cabin, Charles continued, "Now, you mentioned last night about something you desired to speak with us about. What is on your mind, son?"

Peter bit his lip, considering how to begin. As if with sudden determination, he gestured towards the smoke rising from his chimney. "Yes, sir. This may take a little time to work through, and it is much warmer inside. Please, come in." He bounded up the stairs before them and held the door as they followed, though at a slower, more reasonable rate.

They passed through the door he held open, pausing near the fireplace, awaiting his direction.

Pulling a chair out for Mary, Peter requested, "Please, sit down. Mr. Taylor, let me get you a chair." After he and Charles had also taken seats, Peter sat facing his neighbors, preparing to begin.

Curiosity marked itself in Mary's expression, but Charles seemed completely at ease, almost amused. Glancing between the couple, Peter found the words escaping him. Rubbing his chin, he considered how he ought to begin with his explanation. Oddly, he realized that he had been in this situation before, yet he could not find any key to discovering how to broach the subject.

Observing the young man's hesitation, Charles gently prodded, "Take your time, son. Was there something you needed to discuss with us about our family? One of our children?"

Peter let his hand fall upon his lap and riveted his eyes upon Charles. "In a way, it does involve all of you, but mainly it concerns your son, William."

Now concern showed itself in Charles' eyes. "Is it something about his character?"

"No sir, not that. I deeply appreciate his friendship, and other than the fact that he is very persuadable, I have nothing I would consider a fault in reference to him." He sighed, "This has to do with what actually happened last week with the stump."

With a determination to leave nothing untold, Peter related the entire story of how he had broken the old wagon tongue, how he had gone to find another one, and how he had discovered the runaways in the shed. He described how William had demanded he tell no one, and that he had kept the knowledge from Henry when they returned to finish the task they had left off. He apologized for not being completely upfront with them, but explained he had only waited as long as he had because of William's words. He had come to them from a desire to be completely honest with them, to be a true friend.

"...I give you my word that I will pass this information to no one else, but I believed I needed to make you aware of what had happened."

The pair opposite offered gentle smiles of encouragement as Peter finished his tale. Chuckling softly, Mary commented, "So you finally discovered that we do more than just speak against slavery."

Peter nodded. "Yes Ma'am. Samuel's grandson Nathan had only recently told me of the Underground, and before our conversation, I had no idea that such an operation even existed. Then when I discovered that you and your family actually take part in that work and hide runaways...it sent my mind spinning."

"Well," Charles conceded, "not all of us. Only James, William, and Jenny know what we do. We felt it was safer to not tell the younger ones, especially considering that a few in particular tend to open their mouths a little too freely."

Smiling softly, though still not entirely at his ease, Peter chuckled, "Henry is a fine boy, and I appreciate him very much, but he does love to talk."

"That he does," Charles agreed, smiling ruefully as he contemplated his youngest son. "Like I was saying, we have only told the older ones, mainly because it was something that we could not keep from them, and they have been able to help us in the work. We have not lied to our younger children, but we have not told them things they do not need to know."

"I understand. William had only said that not all of your family knew of the work, so I was not sure who all was involved with it. To be honest, he had me wondering whether you were aware of it, or whether it was something he was doing secretly alone."

"No, I believe he was only being overly cautious with you, understanding how important and risky this work can be."

"Though I do wish he had told us he knew you had found out about it," interposed Mary, glancing sidelong at her husband.

"As do I," Charles sighed. "He should have realized that I need to be aware of things such as this. I will discuss the matter with him this afternoon. But," he laid his hands upon his knees, "I am curious: why did Nathan tell you of this work? That is, what prompted him to tell of the Underground?"

"He told me," Peter breathed deeply, "because he was trying to recruit me to be a conductor. He did not tell me anything besides what the work would be; he told me no names, no locations, no information that would put anyone in danger. He left before I could give him my answer, but I am afraid that I would not be able to fill that role. I do earnestly wish to see the slaves freed, but I do not know if I can take part in this work."

"I had no idea he was offering such a task to you," Charles wondered. "Of course, I knew Nathan was a part of the work. He has made several runs through our place himself. I am glad to hear that you desire to bring freedom to our oppressed brothers and sisters, but I can appreciate that you have concerns about the work. Is it something about working in secret?"

"Oh no sir, it is not that at all," Peter countered, looking up sharply. "I understand that this is different than the situation with my past. With that, I was presenting myself to be something I was not, holding back information about where I came from. That was a problem with my friendship towards you all. I realize that this matter is different, and why this must be kept secret. As I told him when he presented it to me, I am deeply grateful and honored by the confidence placed in me by the request. I deeply respect and revere your attitude towards slavery, and I am as opposed to the institution as anyone.

"When I was growing up, I had become friends with one of the slave children about my age, and we quickly formed a close bond. I would bring him food I had snuck from the table, or I would share some candy father gave me with him. One day as I talked with him as he worked, the foremen caught us and informed Father of what I was doing." A far off look crept into his eye as he considered the memory. "Father was furious at what I had done, but his anger towards me was incomparable to his fury towards my friend Gabriel. He made me watch as the foreman beat my friend mercilessly with his whip. I have never forgotten that sight. My attitude towards slavery did not change fully at that point, but it was the beginning of the stirrings within me that reached their fulfilment several years later. I know the cruelty that exists in the slave-holding states; I have seen it first hand with my own eyes. And if I could, I would eradicate the institution today without another thought.

"One of the primary reasons for me not accepting the offer, however, is the matter of time. I feel that I would not be able to make the runs that Nathan has asked me to carry out. It would require me to be gone for weeks at a time, and since I have no family to help take care of my farm while I am away, I would not be able to take care of my own place or provide for my own necessities while here in the valley. You may feel that it is not a reason to refrain from such a work, but I know that I cannot make the runs."

"I commend you for having compassion for our fellow men, even if they have a darker skin. We are all created by God and there is no distinction. Your hesitation to make the full runs that he has asked is a valid concern, and I agree with your evaluation. Still, did Nathan tell you that not all conductors make the full run from the cotton land all the way into the North?"

"No sir," Peter replied slowly. "He only asked if I would be willing to lead the slaves to freedom."

Charles nodded. "I see. There are many individuals in your same situation who are not able to leave their steads for weeks on end, so they make shorter runs between stations. They might lead them between several houses, or just to the next one. William has been the main one to do that for us, but if you were desiring to take part in the work, we would be pleased and honored to have you do that between our home and the next house, taking turns making the runs with William." He surveyed the young man. "But from your manner, there seems to be something else weighing upon your heart, is there not?"

Peter lifted his eyes to meet the gaze of his neighbor, then began slowly, "Yes sir, there is. Please do not hear anything that I am about to say as anything disparaging against you or your family. I deeply respect the decision that you have made. I do desire to help with bringing freedom to slaves, I earnestly do. I know that what you have described for me is a capacity that I could fill. However, I do not know if I can, in good conscience that is.

"You see, even when I thought Nathan meant for me to make the complete runs, I wondered that if I was to help in the Underground work, whether I would be giving assistance to those who were breaking the law of the land. We are commanded to help return slaves to their masters, and while I would not follow that, I do not know that I can go against it. Paul says in Romans that we are to be subject to the governing authorities, but I feel that assisting in the Underground would be to disregard the authorities that God has set up for America."

Nodding slowly, Charles acknowledged the young man's concerns. "I can see that. I admire your desire to follow the Word of God; it reflects your heart to obey the Lord. But," he leaned forward in his chair, "what does the Bible say about what a man is to do when the law of man goes against the law of God?"

"Sir?"

"Do you remember, I think it is in the fifth chapter of Acts, when Peter and the other apostles are brought before the Pharisees and commanded to not preach the Gospel anymore to the people? When Peter hears their demands, he said, 'We ought to obey God rather than men.' That has been mine and Mary's answer to this dilemma, as I am sure it has been for Nathan.

"The government has no right to force an entire race of people into servitude for something they cannot help, especially for the color of their skin. Slavery in America is worse than servitude. Men, women, and children are treated worse than dogs, told they have no rights to do anything other than to work the fields of rich whites. That is contrary to the Word of God. As Paul would say, 'there is no partiality between' any race of people, since we are all one in Christ Jesus. There can be no slavery like our country permits, and that is why we chose to disregard any law Washington may produce that may say otherwise."

"We know that the Bible talks about slaves," Mary added, "but slavery in America does not abide by what the Word of God sets forth for how masters are to treat those under their charge."

"Exactly," Charles affirmed. "And consider this: no human can own another as if they are mere pieces of property. Yes, the Bible contains descriptions of men who had slaves, but it was not an ownership like these plantation owners claim they have. I have heard some people claim that helping runaways is akin to thievery, but the two are entirely separate issues. Men are not property, so they cannot be stolen. Men are all the same in God's sight, but we must fight against any who claim otherwise!"

"Fight? As in taking up arms?" Peter inquired, surprised by the man's words.

"Excuse me," he smiled gently. "That sounds like something William or Nathan might say. I mean resist and oppose. We do not resort to violence unless we must to defend ourselves. Does this answer your problem?"

"In part, but to be honest, I am beginning to be confused. I have heard you chastise James for his passionate speeches about a Southern nation, saying that we have no quarrel with the government in Washington, but yet you just spoke of how we must defy our government who is making ungodly and unbiblical legislation. I admit, I fail to see the correlation."

"Your question is valid," Charles admitted. "What I mean with James is that we still have an obligation to obey the government God has set up in all matters that do not contradict the Bible. There are no laws in America, besides the ones concerning slavery, that do that, as far as I understand it. We must work to bring freedom to slaves, but we must obey the government in all other areas. Even if the Southern states were to form their own nation, slavery would still be a practice inherent to the land, probably even more deeply rooted than it is now. We have no reason to desire our own nation. We only strive to follow the Lord under the one we have now."

CHAPTER 7

Rising from his bowed position, Peter felt a sense of peace settle upon him. As his country moved closer and closer to war, he had been driven increasingly nearer to his God. He poured out his fears, his concerns to the Lord, begging for guidance and wisdom, interceding for his country and the rift between the states.

And as he had been confronted with the offer of first Nathan and then the Taylors, he found himself seeking the Lord through prayer even more. The struggle had not been easy. He despised himself for his indecisiveness, but he needed to be sure he was making the right choice before he settled upon his decision.

Charles' words seemed sound and filled with wisdom, but the prospect of working to resist the government in secret troubled him for a time. Yet as he had prayed and meditated on his options, he felt himself drawn towards the only decision he felt left open to him. Issues, problems, and difficulties lay on both sides, but he knew that his faith demanded he make the only decision consistent with his profession.

Taking the metal rod in his hand, Peter stirred the fire, pushing the logs back on top of one another. He knew Charles awaited his answer, and as he grabbed his coat on his way out of his cabin, he turned with rigid determination in the direction of the Taylor's farm.

As the wind blew bitingly through his coat while he strode down the country road, Peter felt his mind drift to the scene of the runaways he had found it the cabin, then turn to the shacks—if they even deserved the name—of the slaves on his family's plantation. Compassion and sorrow welled up in his spirit as he considered the sufferings the slaves went through in their limited protection from the elements, especially during the brutal months of winter. His contemplations only solidified his decision in his mind.

Turning into his neighbor's yard, he found Mary taking in clothes from off the line. As usual, a quilt hung upon the far side of one of the wires. As he approached, he raised a hand in greeting. "Hello, Mrs. Taylor," he called.

"Afternoon, Peter," she returned cheerily. "How are you?"

"Fine, thank you. And yourself?"

"Doing well, but my! Ain't this quite the cold snap settling in?"

"Yes ma'am," he chuckled. "It sure is." He slowed his pace as he neared the basket she had laid upon the ground. "I was wondering where I might find Mr. Taylor at this afternoon."

"I believe he is up at the barn with some of the boys," she replied, curiosity filling her eyes as she cocked her head slightly to one side. "Is there something you needed him for?"

Peter smiled encouragingly. "I wanted to let him know my answer to…his proposition."

"Will…" her brow knitted together with intense interest, "are you going to accept it?"

Peter nodded affirmingly. "Yes ma'am. I intend to."

"Oh, I am so glad," she exulted, her expression brightening. "We had been praying the Lord would give you wisdom for your decision, regardless of whether you choose to join us or not. He is up at the barn. I know he will be so pleased to discuss this more fully with you."

"Thank you," Peter smiled, tipping his hat towards her as he turned in the direction she had indicated.

As Mary had thought, he found Charles cleaning out the barn along with William, George, and Robert. The men exchanged warm greetings and passing comments about the weather and their work, yet Peter refrained from referencing the errand upon which he had come, remembering that Charles had said that not all of his children knew of the Underground work.

Sensing the young man restraining a burden within him, Charles gazed intently at Peter. With a nod of understanding, he turned towards George. "How 'bout you and Robert run up the house real quick and see what time Shawna's planning on having supper on the table, while I talk with Peter, hear?"

"Yes sir," George complied, laying his pitchfork against the wall and leaving with Robert to fulfill his father's request.

Once they were passed out of the barn, Charles continued to Peter, "I think It seems that you have something on your mind, am I right?"

"Yes sir. I wanted to let you know my decision to your request the other day." Forming the words in him slowly so as to be sure they came out as he intended them to, he explained, "I have been doing a powerful amount of studying on the subject the past few days, and I have realized that no matter what I do, this country is headed for war, sure as Abraham Lincoln is going to be our President. I also know that I want to help free the slaves now, and regardless of what happens with this war, we are still going to have to figure out a plan of how to do it." He turned his full attention upon the man standing before him. "I want to be a part of that effort now. I don't want to wait for the government to heal this breach in unity between the two halves of the nation, and then work out some bureaucratic deal over the next thirty, forty years to free the slaves. I have considered the consequences of both waiting and of taking part now, and I know that no matter what might happen, I must help my brothers and sisters escape from this tyranny on the plantations."

The lines of tension fading into a bright, welcoming smile, Charles offered an outstretched hand to Peter. "That's what I was hopin' you'd say."

Springing forward, William shook his friend's hand vigorously, his own smile matching that of his father. "Pete, it is so good to have you with us!"

"Hold on now," Peter laughed softly at his enthusiasm. "I do not know in detail what I am to do, and I have not even started yet. You all have been carrying out this work for years, so I would hardly say I am with you yet."

"Oh, details," William laughed. "Who cares 'bout them anyhow?"

"You might be surprised," his father chuckled wryly. "Yet to your point, Peter, we will show you all you will need to learn. William has made the run several times, and I know he will be more than willing to go over the route with you, giving you the *details* of our work."

"Yes sir, I most definitely would. What cha' got going on this evening?"

"Not anything that I recall right now," Peter mused. "I would hate to pull you away from anything you need to do here though."

"We will have the work finished here shortly, so tonight will be fine." He clapped Peter on the shoulder. "It is so good to know you will be working with us now. I'll see ya here in a bit."

■■■■■■■■■■■■■■■■■■■■■■■■■■■■■■■■■■■■■■■

True to his word, William appeared at Peter's cabin shortly after supper, a map tucked under his arm and wide grin plastered upon his face. Laying the papers upon the table, the two young men bent over the maps, discussing routes and other aspects of being a conductor late into the night. William pointed out different particulars of guiding, such as how to stay upon an unmarked trail in the dark and the balance of leading and watching.

When asked how accurate of a shot he was, Peter looked up with a start. "Will, we are talking about helping slaves escape, not joining an army."

"I know that. But have you considered what will happen when a slave catcher comes upon your group as you lead them through the woods? As terrible as it is to say, when it comes down to it, someone may be killed. It could be you, or it could be one of the slaves, but someone might be shot on sight even." He looked up with intensity at the young man. "Peter, you don't give them the opportunity. You stay in the darkest parts, you keep quiet. But if it comes down to it, and it is their life or one of those in your charge, you shoot, you understand me?"

"You are asking me to kill a man?"

"No, not exactly. Like you said, this is not the army. What I am asking is that even if it means you have to protect the runaways you are leading by putting a bullet in a slave catcher, you do that. I do not mean you have to kill him, but you stop him. He will not hesitate putting one in you if it means he can take those men and woman back to collect a reward. I know you hate to think about having to do that, but it is something we have to be prepared for."

He folded the map, smoothed it with his hand, and tucked it under his arm once again, his eyes coming to rest upon the rifle set above the fireplace. "You take that rifle with you every time. It is your protector."

"No," Peter countered, "God is my Protector. I trust in Him to guide me and to give me strength and wisdom as I will lead the runaways."

"You are right," William conceded. "You are right. I agree that the Lord is the One we trust, but He has given us a mind to think and hands to defend, and there are times where He asks us to use them. That's all I am saying." Striding over to the rack by the door, William placed his hat snuggly upon his head. Turning again to his host, he offered his hand in parting. "Pete, I can't tell you how glad I am that you are joining us."

Taking his hand in his own firm grip, Peter replied, "I pray I am making the right decision, and I believe that I am. I do have one final question though. How am I going to know when I need to lead the slaves? I do not stop by your place every day, but is that something I need to be doing?"

"Oh, you don't have to do that...unless you wanted to," William chuckled. "All you have to do is look for the quilts."

CHAPTER EIGHT

"...And so, just past that clump of trees yonder is the path to the Foster's on up by Ford's Creek," Charles gestured towards a small patch of oaks that seem to bulge out from the tree line behind the old shed where the runaways hid. On his way home from Samuel's the day following his instruction from William, Peter had turned in to the Taylor's yard as he passed and, directed by Henry, found Charles just coming back from inspecting one of the family's fields. William had told him to come by the house and see where the path he would take lay in proximity to the shed and other such final details, Peter explained. Charles nodded, then called Peter to follow him.

After putting his horse into the stall, Charles had led Peter to the old shed, explaining along the way details of how they were able to provide the runaways with blankets, food, and even clothes occasionally.

Though he could not form into words what he felt inside, Peter's heart beat harder as they had approached the outbuilding, saw the paths he would be leading the runaways along, and heard Charles detailed explanation. Before he had discovered the slaves that fateful afternoon, the idea of the Underground was only a rumor he had heard occasionally, but nothing more. But there on that hill, it had become real to him, and as he stood there with his new knowledge of the inner workings of the secret network, he could hardly believe he was now actually a part of it. He was persuaded he had chosen the only option he could make, seeing the things he had witnessed as a child and heard the stories he had, and though an unsettledness remained about what lay ahead in the future, there was no regret in Peter's spirit.

"I suppose that William has explained the rest to you already," Charles turned back to his companion. "Once they are in the woods, they are your charge."

Peter nodded solemnly. "Yes sir."

Returning the nod, Charles started back towards the cabin in the plain below them. "So, do you have any questions about any of this?"

"Well, I do have a few. Your son mentioned something last night about looking for the quilts, but he did not elaborate on the specifics, only noting that certain ones were signals for the slaves, and would be for me as well."

"He is right there. To the casual observer, they look like family quilts, unidentifiable from the next one. But to the runaways, they are the signs they are looking for when a station is safe to enter, when it is too dangerous to come to the house, among other such signals. We could put a particular one out on the line whenever a group of runaways come to us, and when you see it, you will know that there is a run to make that night."

"I always thought it was odd that there always seemed to be one hanging out to dry," Peter smiled. "I had mentioned it to Jenny one day, but she merely said that your wife desired to have them aired out on a regular basis, and with all of your children still at home, I did not pay much attention to it."

"Did she now?" the older man chuckled, a twinkle in his eye barely noticeable. "Well, I suppose that would be one way to explain it, but like I described to you, there is much more to it than that."

"If you do not mind me asking, how did you settle upon using the quilts as messages? I know Nathan Kouffers travels around rather frequently with this work, so did he introduce you to the quilt signals?"

"Nathan? Oh no," Charles shook his head, his faint smile widening in amusement. "We had been hiding slaves long before I met the young man. I am not sure who started the idea of using quilt patterns as signals, but it has been used for years, and it is quite an effective system. Now, is there anything else on your mind before we reach the house?"

"Yes sir, there is, but I am not sure how to say it."

"Take your time, son. I want to clear any concerns you may have."

Peter thanked him, then lapsed into a momentary silence, the pace of the two slowing as they continued their descent of the slope towards the Taylor's cabin. Stealing a furtive glance towards his companion, Peter began, "It is not precisely a concern, but I was curious about James. I know the work that you and your wife do, you told me of how Jenny helps with the provisions for the runaways, and I know that William leads them to the next station. Yet I have not heard you speak of James and the part he plays in all of this."

"James," Charles sighed, a note of sorrow filling the forlorn sound, "James would never betray us, but he does not fully support our work with the Underground. Do not misunderstand me, he believes that slavery is wrong. Not as strongly as you and I feel about it, but he does consider it an evil of our nation. However, the lure of a Southern nation that would allow life to continue as an agricultural society instead of an industrial one like the North has captured his attention, and he is afraid what helping slaves escape from the plantations might do to the South. Quite honestly, he is persuaded that it will cripple it, and he may be right. He claims that to remove the slave labor now would be to set up the South for failure when war comes, and he is not willing to face that.

"I fear for my son, Peter. He has always been enraptured with the Southern culture, but recent events have only fanned the fire within him. And having friends like the Mason's and the Jones' certainly has not helped matters any. I do not know what he will do in the future, but he has not been willing to help us by leading the runaways to the next station."

He sighed heavily once again, then murmured softly, "And he is only continuing to grow worse."

Before he left the Taylor's that evening, Peter had been shown the quilt he was to look for to know when runaways had come to the cabin. He had a clear view of the clothes line as he passed their home on the country lane, and he began to search for the specific pattern each time their home came into his sight on his return from the cabinet shop each evening. The Taylors had informed him that there was no pattern or rhythm for when the runaways would come. Sometimes two groups would only be separated by a matter of a few days. Other times, a few weeks might pass by. He always had to be ready to make his run during any night.

Following Nathan's instructions, he had written to the young man and informed him that he had decided to try his hand at surveying, though still continuing to work as a cabinet maker. He was not sure how to describe the fact that he was only making local runs, but he hoped Nathan would infer the meaning from his words.

Still unsure of how much information his employer knew of the underground work in Chesson, Peter refrained from telling Samuel anything about his decision, not even referencing the secret work. Whether from a lack of suspicion, or from a desire to remain silent, Peter couldn't tell, but Samuel never discussed the subject either. He had offhandedly made the comment about knowing that illnesses were more prevalent in winter, and if Peter needed to come in several hours later, not to trouble himself about it. Peter suspected that there was more to the suggestion than Samuel verbalized, but he gratefully accepted the offer.

Peter placed the last of the chisels away and turned to face his employer. "Is there anything else, Mr. Kouffers?"

Hanging his apron upon its peg by the door, Samuel gently shook his head. "Naw, son. I believe that is everything." He turned to face the young man, concern in his voice, inquired, "Are you alright, Peter? You have seemed a little distracted all day, but you do not look too well now. Are you feeling poorly?"

"No sir, I am fine. I beg your forgiveness for today. There are a few things weighing upon my spirit, but I did not mean for them to take me from my work."

"Oh, you did fine. Your mind only seemed to be focused upon something other than what your hands were occupied with. Is it the threat of what may happen to our nation that is bothering you again?"

Peter nodded. "It is, sir."

"I am concerned with that as well, Peter, but we do not need to allow it to cause us to fear. There has been no declaration of war, and though it is a possibility, we do not know that things will actually reach that point. The Senators and Congressmen may be able to restore this break that has occurred further south. At any rate, prayer is what we must devote ourselves to, not fear. The good Lord is still in control; none of this has taken Him by surprise. Take your worries to Him, lay them at His feet, and follow Him wherever He leads."

"Thank you, sir. I have been, but I confess, it is a struggle not to give into worry. If it does come to war, I do not know what I will do. If the North was to move against Virginia, I think I would readily take up arms in our state's defense. Not out of hatred, but to protect our home land. Yet I do not know if I can because of the Bible's teaching about submitting to the government, and especially now with...oh, just that."

A hint of curiosity at the half-finished reason flickering in his eye, Samuel returned, "It is a honest concern, and I am glad to hear that you are evaluating yourself. But Peter, we do not know if war will even come. Let us trust the Lord, praying for His guidance. If it comes to that point, I know He will make it clear to you if you seek Him. But for now, we need to focus on praying for healing and restoration for our land. We can consider what we will do, but we must not let it become worry. Trust the Lord for each day. He will guide you."

"Thank you, sir." Peter smiled softly at the wise council of the older man. "I will."

Samuel's face softened reassuringly. "I believe you, son. I will be praying as well. I'll lock up here in a moment. You go on home."

"Yes sir. Good night." He exchanged his apron for his hat upon the rack, and with a final nod to Samuel, began his journey home.

He appreciated the wisdom of his employer. Samuel often acted as an anchor for Peter whenever he became caught up in a concern, making it larger than what it might actually be. He would encourage him to always seek the Lord, but he would also offer council from his own experience. It would never supersede the Lord and his Word by any means, but Samuel would give it, offering Peter another perspective he might not have considered before.

Peter was still contemplating Samuel's words as he rounded the last bend in the lane in his approach to the Taylor's home. His eye absently glanced towards the clothes line. The specified quilt had not appeared since he had accepted his work, but it was hanging out there that afternoon, stopping Peter dead in his tracks. A sensation similar to the one he had experienced when Charles detailed his work washed over him. It was real. It was the night he was to make his first run as a conductor.

Pulling himself into action, Peter dug his shoes into the ground and ran for his cabin, as fast as his boots would allow him to race, that is. Once he had retrieved his rifle, powder, and shot, he would be back, for William had reminded him that he would be worthless if he did not have a weapon to defend himself and his charges with. Although Peter did not place as much faith in his rifle as the other young man did, he did believe that he had a responsibility to protect those he would be guiding. And so he ran.

Bursting into his cabin, he grabbed his satchel he kept his firing caps and cartridges in and slung it over his shoulder. With a swift motion, he lifted the Springfield rifle from its resting place and tucked it under his arm. Swinging his cabin's door closed behind him, he took off across the field that separated his land from the Taylor's.

A line of woods divided the two properties, and Peter plunged into it, swiping branches away before him with his free hand, ducking those he missed, and leaping over fallen trees and brush that cluttered the ground beneath him. As Peter broke through the last line of brush that separated his land from the Taylors', barreling towards his neighbor's cabin, a figure sauntering up the path from the lane arrested his steps. Seth Mason strode along the path towards the cabin, seemingly without a care in the world. Though Peter searched desperately for a place to conceal his presence, Seth's eye had already found him.

With an attempt to cover his sneer, Seth called, "Peter, where the dickens are you headed, running around looking all the world like Daniel Boone?"

"Evening, Seth," Peter replied guardedly, unsure of how to explain his strange entrance. "Er, have you seen William around?"

"No, I was just up at the mill looking for him and his father, but the place was all closed up. But if you are looking for someone to play with, I think Henry might be a better option."

Before Peter had a chance to respond, the front door opened and James' voice drifted across the January air. "Hello, Seth. Didn't expect to see you this evening."

"Oh," Seth shrugged, "my folks sent me over to invite you and yer family for dinner after meeting in the morning. I was telling Peter here that I went by the mill, but y'all had already left."

At the mention of his neighbor, James' face suddenly furrowed with concern and his eye searched for the young man. "Peter?"

"Over here, James." Peter stepped around the side of the cabin into his friend's vision.

"He has quite the get-up this evening, does he not?" Seth commented, smirking.

Ignoring the insult, James continued to Peter, "I don't think William was planning on going hunting tonight, but I will let him and father know. I am sure that they would like to say a word to you, anyway."

"Oh, I...I understand. I'll just wait around back for them."

"I'll tell them. Seth, why don't you come on in. Shawna's got quite the spread, but that's nothing unusual."

As Seth followed James inside, Peter slinked around the back of the cabin, chastising himself for his fool-hardiness in his actions. *Yet,* his mind argued with him, *how did you know Seth was going to be calling?* Still, he could not take another chance like that again.

After a few moments, the back door parted and William appeared, his own face tight with concern. He whispered, "Follow me."

He led the way towards the barn, continuing in hushed tones, "I had no idea Seth was going to be calling."

"Neither did I," Peter returned, equally hushed in volume. "But Will, why are we headed this way? The shed's up on—"

"Hush!" William grabbed Peter's gesturing hand and shoved it back to his side. Stealing a glance behind them towards the cabin, he explained, "You can never be too careful with Seth. Seeing you with your rifle and everything has made him suspicious, and I am not about to give him any idea of something being up with the old cabin."

"I'm sorry."

"Aw, you didn't know he was coming, and I know you didn't mean anything by pointing. Just try to watch it, hear? People's lives might depend on it."

The two young men lapsed into silence as William chose a path that meandered across the fields, then doubled back along the wood line towards the old shed where the runaways hid. When they reached the door, William rapped upon the wooden panels three times before opening it slightly and motioning Peter inside, following his neighbor in at the young man's heels.

The interior was dimly lit by the last remnants of the fading sun forcing its way through the cracks in the shed's wall. The same old farm implements lay in one corner, and behind a few old barrels and lumber, six sets of eyes peered back at Peter and William.

William laid a hand on Peter shoulder and explained, "Friends, this is Peter. He is going to lead you to the next station. I would trust him with my life, and I know he will give his own to protect yours. He knows these woods like the back of his hand. I have full confidence in him." Then turning to Peter, he nodded towards the small door on the far side of the room. "That opens right next to the path, but I'm sure Pa already showed you that."

He faced the runaways who had risen and stood expectantly. "My family and I will be praying for you. God speed." With a parting grip of Peter's hand, he slipped out the door they had entered.

Peter gazed at the six Negro men and women who had embarked on their way to freedom. They were placing their lives in his hands. *No, not my hands,* he chided himself. *God will protect us.*

He stepped to the small door and pulled it open. "Let's go."

CHAPTER NINE

The sun had just begun to pierce the darkness as Peter had sprawled himself upon his cot that first night after he had led the runaways. He had done it. He was officially a part of the underground work, and there was no turning back now. Discussing how not to repeat his absurd arrival, Peter and the Taylors had determined that he would simply make his way to the small cabin without having to stop by their home first. It would alleviate any suspicion, and since the forest wrapped around their properties, Peter could slip through without being noticed.

And so their routine had settled in. Peter would watch every day for the signal quilt, and once it appeared, he would make his way in a casual manner to his cabin to avoid any suspicion from anyone else who might happen to be on the road, then take off on his midnight run, dragging himself back home in the wee hours of the morning. As Charles had told him, sometimes days would elapse between runs, other times a period of a few weeks would pass. As he was trading with William in terms of whom led each group of runaways, he only had to guide every other band that came, so they were spaced out even more so than usual for him. But it did not matter to Peter. He rejoiced that he was able to take part in the work in even the small way he did, and though his concerns for the future still remained, he would always cast an eager eye to the Taylor's clothes line each evening as he strolled down the lane on his way home from a day's work with Samuel.

The weeks quickly faded into months, the temperatures rising steadily, bringing the first signs of spring to the Chesson Valley. Peter enjoyed his walks to and from work even more with the warmer weather, appreciating the symbols of new life that his eye would find in nature.

But as the oaks, hickories, and gum trees began shooting forth their leaves, the Confederate States of America was shooting forth her own signs of life. South Carolina had struck the match with its secession in December of the previous year. Now Alabama, Mississippi, Georgia, Florida...so many states had joined her. With each state that transferred its allegiance to the Confederacy, James Taylor wound up tighter and tighter over states' rights. He was nearly furious that almost the entire South had joined the Confederacy and, still, Virginia held out. As was his usual habit, William joined his opinion to that of his older brother, becoming swept up in James' fervent passion. Still, William's attitude surprised Peter, considering the young man's involvement with the Underground. He would have to ask him about it sometime.

When the news had arrived on Monday about Fort Sumter, it was as if someone had set off a bundle of dynamite in the Chesson valley. The farms, homesteads, and the small town were ablaze with the talk of that fateful day: April 12, 1861. Up until that point, the talk of a Southern nation had been a dream.

A very real dream, but still a dream. But once the South Carolinians had actually fired upon a federal fort and brought about its subsequent surrender, the dream became a reality—one simultaneously longed for and feared.

As the tensions continued to mount, and Peter found men like himself and Charles Taylor with their views upon the government becoming a rapidly deceasing percentage of the valley, he realized even more precautions were called for. Their views against slavery had not caused any suspicions among their neighbors, at least not so far as Peter could tell, but he did worry about what might be aroused by his opposition to the increasing tide of Confederate fervor. He was a rather reclusive type of character, and aside from the Taylors and Samuel Kouffers, he tended to remain alone. If he continued his free and easy manner around others who held similar unpopular views, he was afraid of how some of their stanchly confederate neighbors might perceive their friendship.

And so, Peter had begun to distance himself even more from those around him. The change was gradual, but he accepted fewer and fewer invitations to supper, even from the Taylors. He still maintained a cordial attitude with his acquaintances and neighbors, but his withdraw made it harder to sustain close relationships with other members of their community. He was not entirely persuaded that it was the right decision, but he considered it preferable to what might happen if he did not change.

The Choice

Peter clicked the reigns on the horse's back as he rode home in his small wagon, his mind considering his recent choices in light of the changing atmosphere of the valley. It was hard to believe that it had actually been one full week since Fort Sumter had been fired upon. He reflected on what the consequences of such an action might entail. Regardless of what the long-term results were, war had actually come to their nation. It was shameful that his countrymen had allowed their differing views to be carried to such an extent, but they had done it and they could not change it. The question that remained was what to do now.

"PETER!" He whirled around to face the owner of the voice that had cried out to him, interrupting his musings. His sharp eye quickly spotted two riders leaning low in their saddles, racing their steeds toward him at an impressive speed. He pulled back the reigns and brought his cart to a halt and awaited the duo who had recently hailed him.

As the two figures drew closer, Peter noticed that it was William and Seth. William straightened in his saddle and began furiously waving a newspaper above his head, a smile splitting his face from ear to ear. "Peter – they've done it! They have really done it!"

The two riders drew their mounts up alongside Peter's cart, both horses and riders breathing hard from their gallop. Peter questionly surveyed his two friends, curious to know what news called for such enthusiasm and recklessness. "William, what is it? Who has done what?"

Still panting hard from his ride, William handed the paper to him and explained, "Virginia, my good sir! Virginia has finally joined the Confederate States of America!"

With trepidation at what he might read, Peter received the paper and scanned the front-page article. William was right, Virginia had seceded. He couldn't believe it. He knew that many in the state's government had wanted to make the decision for some time now, but he had never considered that it might actually happen.

The ramifications began to sink upon him, twisting his gut as it were, dread swelling up inside. Whether he liked it or not, he and his neighbors were now part of the southern nation, and if something radical did not occur, they would be at war with their northern states.

Peter glanced up furtively, his spirit sinking even more as he surveyed William's joyous face. Did he realize what it might mean for their work in the Underground? They were now right at the border of their country, only increasing the fervor of the slave catchers and intensifying their search for runaways before they escaped across into the North. The Fugitive Slave Law had been horrible enough—what new legislation might the Confederate government enact?

Peter handed the paper back to William, shaking his head in disbelief. "I, uh, I never thought they would actually do it."

"Well, you had better start believing it" Seth cut in, studying Peter in his habitual suspicious manner. "They've done it, and Virginia has finally taken her rightful stand in the Confederacy! She should have been one of the first to follow Carolina's decision, but now at last we have. Don't you see what this might mean?"

"No, I don't think any of us do," Peter uncomfortably fingered the reins of his wagon. "We do not know what the Confederate government might do. We do not know if this will invoke a civil war in our nation—"

"No, you mean a war between the *two* nations," Seth corrected doggedly, his eyes narrowing slightly.

As Peter returned his gaze, he realized that he was no longer a loyal citizen of the Union: he was a rebel who sympathized with the enemy. He scrambled for a reply to avert Seth's suspicious gaze.

"Uh, Will...have you told James yet?"

"No, we ain't found him yet," William shook his head. "We were on our way to find him back at the house when we came across you and wanted to share the news." He observed the glares Seth leveled at Peter, realizing that more was transpiring than a mere difference of enthusiasm over the news. "Uh, Seth. We had better get going. James will holler like crazy when he hears this!"

Straightening in his saddle, Seth replied, though his eyes never left Peter, "I know he will. There are those in the valley who truly appreciate the significance of this." With a tip of his hat, he whipped his horse and sped off down the lane. William sheepishly smiled, then turned to follow the other young man, leaving Peter alone with the dread settling in his heart.

■■■

The dull tapping of a mallet against a chisel wafted throughout the cabinet shop as Samuel carved the intricate fingers of a joint on the end of a board upon his work bench. Though the Underground was never broached between him and Peter, Samuel shared Peter's concern for what now lay ahead of them. War was fast approaching, and the subject was just as distasteful to him as it was to Peter, though it affected him in a different way. He was beyond the years of military service, and though he prayed it would not come to it, the older man feared that Peter might be called upon to join any military that would be raised in that event.

Yet Samuel cautioned Peter to not let that concern turn into worry or fear of the future. The Lord was still in control, he would remind his apprentice, and He would lead them in what lay before them. Furthermore, a war had not started. Shots had been fired at Fort Sumter, yes, but as of yet no invading force had been called for by either country. That time might come, but fretful worry would solve nothing.

Pausing in his work, Samuel blew the small shavings from the table's top. Satisfied with his work, he laid aside his tools and deposited the narrow board beside its pair, which rested against a pole supporting the low roof of the shop. "I tell you the truth, Peter," he wagged his head as he marked out a joint on the next board, "it seems that these folks that want the most work done demand it be finished in the quickest amount of time."

"How's that, sir?" Peter glanced up from the spindles he was depositing in the seat of a dining room chair he was restoring.

"Oh, this set for the Jones' place. He was insistent that it be made such a particular way, and he acted as if I had no other jobs I had already started upon, as if I was wiling away hours here at the shop and merely waiting for a project," he chuckled. "Not that we are covered up or anything, but we still have these other jobs to complete. And these people who are looking for pieces of more practical value are not bothered by time, appreciating the work as we get it done without rushing us—have you noticed that before?"

"No sir, I can't say that I have paid much attention to it, yet as you mention it, it does seem to be that way as I consider some of the recent jobs we had done."

"You take Jones here. Just yesterday 'forenoon after meeting, he was on me like a hawk, a'pestering away at me about when we might get it finished up. It was annoying that he didn't believe me when I told him we would complete it as soon as we were able, but to bring it up on the Lord's Day..." he took up his tools once again.

"I think he has it in his head that everyone ought to give him priority."

"I believe you're right there, son. And not just with work, neither. He expects everyone to agree with his views. I avoid many subjects with the man, for he makes me angry the way he carries on so. It is hard to treat him like I ought to as a follower of Christ, but adding to it by discussing particular matters certainly does not aid me in that."

"I have the same trouble," Peter sighed, contemplating the volatile issue that was the subject of so many conversations in Chesson.

"You talk with Jones that much?"

"O no sir, not with him. With the Mason's oldest son, Seth."

"Hah!"

Peter looked up sharply at Samuel's outburst. Despite their having mentioned the young man in question in the past, he had not known his employer shared his aversion for the young man.

Noticing Peter's abrupt change of attention, Samuel explained, "That boy is so full of his arrogant...never mind. He is so stuck upon himself that a fellow can't have a five minute conversation with him without realizing that Seth believes he about hung the moon and all the stars 'long with it. One of these days he is going to trip up and land face-first in the mud, and if he don't fall himself, some fella's going to sock him right in the mouth. The boy's had it coming for years, but it is only getting worse, considering recent events."

"Seth does rub me the wrong way, I admit, yet I don't know that I would call him a boy. He is nearly—"

"I don't care how old he is in years; he's still just a boy in his heart. When he grows up to realize life ain't all 'bout him and begins to understand a little humility, then he'll be a man. But 'til that time, Seth's still just a boy."

Samuel brushed the sawdust from the board. "Before I get myself all worked up with what I'm a saying, let's discuss something else, hear? I have a trouble with saying things that don't have no need being said. Anyway, I heard from Nathan the other day."

"Really? How is he making out?" Peter hadn't seen the other young man since before he had first joined the Underground work, and it had been a few months since they had received any word from him.

"He finds himself tolerable enough, though his work is beginning to slack off here as of late. He says his family's doing well and that the planting went fine. Tensions down there seem to be about as bad as they are up in these parts, judging from the letter." Samuel's voice suddenly turned grave, a shadow beginning to darken his face. "He was also saying something else that concerns me, Peter. He writes that he is planning on joining the military when the call is given. It is not that I think he is wrong for making that decision, if that is how the Lord is leading him. What worries me is how eagerly he seemed to write of his choice, and that he has made that decision at this time when there is no declared war concerning his state. Does that make any sense?"

"It does, sir."

Samuel nodded. "It is not for me to judge the intentions of another, but I do know that the Lord takes no pleasure in the death of the wicked, and that violence is something He commands us to avoid. War is not something we should enter into lightly, or even with anticipation. Though many talk of the glory of war, it is a horrible, cruel thing, something so many your age have no capacity to fathom. While I do not believe there will be a long conflict if a war should engage between the North and the South, it still does not negate the sorrow of men killing one another because of a dispute. That is my hesitation with Nathan. There is a time for war, the Bible says, but my grandson's attitude towards this issue concerns me, for he has not shared his reasons for his decision."

Silently working for a moment, Peter considered Samuel's words. The news that Nathan was even considering joining the Confederate military was a fact that took him completely unawares. Not that he knew the young man as well as he did William, Peter still thought he understood Nathan's opinion of a Confederacy. He could not see how fighting for the Confederacy was compatible with work on the Underground—had Nathan reversed his views on that work as well? Peter would have expected this decision to have been made by Seth and James, or possibly even William, but definitely not Nathan.

Reaching for another small spindle, Peter glanced towards his employer. "Had Nathan mentioned before that he was considering making that decision?"

"No, and that is one thing that surprises me. As I said, there is a time for war, and if Nathan's heart is true, then I raise no objection. It is the suddenness of this decision that has surprised me."

"You believe that there would be a reason to join the Confederacy? If it came to war, I mean."

Samuel paused, avoiding meeting the gaze of his young employee. "It is not for me to say what any particular man should or should not do in this situation, but to answer your question, I do feel that there are particular circumstances where it would be compatible with a person's faith for him to join the military."

"But would that not be rebelling against the rightful authority that God has put in place?"

"If our nation—for that is what the South is now—if our nation was to invade the North right now, then you are correct in your evaluation. It would be a rebellion, even more so than what we are engaged in now.

"However, let us say for the sake of argument that the North was to invade the South, whether it be here, or Kentucky, or wherever. At that point, things would be different. If the Federal army came into the capital, arrested the leaders of this rebellion and that was as far as things went, we would have no quarrel with them. But if that army was to invade the South and begin destroying property, whether by war or plunder, and killing their brethren, then men would have a responsibility to take up arms in defense."

"But would that still not be resisting the rightful government, the government in Washington?"

"There would be those who would feel that way, certainly. But consider this—what if a man was blessed of God with a family and a farm to raise that family on. What if some men came, and for reasons that he had no control over, began to destroy that farm and threaten the life of his family. Would that man not have a responsibility to defend his home and family? That is what may happen here. May happen, mind you. I did not say that it would. If it came to that situation, then I do feel that a man has a duty to take up arms and resist those who would invade this land."

To defend.... That was a reason Peter had not seen before. "But if that man was defending his farm, would he not do that himself? Why would he join the army?"

"That is a question you will have to decide for yourself," Samuel smiled softly, compassionately realizing the struggle within the young man. "There will be those who choose to stay on their own, try to defend their own personal property against those who would ransack and plunder it. But then there are those who would deem that it would be better to join with others in a united effort to resist such an invasion. One man against a regiment of hungry soldiers is a poorly-matched fight, Peter. Yet the issue of conscience of joining the Confederacy is a matter that someone else cannot determine for you. Remember what I always tell you when difficult decisions arise?"

"Seek the Lord, pray, and be obedient to what He has shown you."

Samuel smiled. "That is right. I pray that Nathan has been doing that. If he has and the Lord has led him to this decision, I have no quarrel with him. I urge you to do the same, but still remember that we are not at war yet. The Lord may yet reconcile the South to the North before any blood is shed. I pray God that it may be the case. Still, the Lord calls us to consider our ways and to prepare for the future. As you do that, I caution you to beware of allowing yourself from being swayed by other men in the valley, even from me. The Lord must be the One who guides you, not man. Seek Him, Peter. Seek Him earnestly."

CHAPTER TEN

"I do not know about any of the rest of y'all, but speaking for myself, I'm going up as soon as the call comes in for volunteers," announced Seth Mason as he laid the package on the General Store's counter. When his uncle was short on employees for whatever reason, he would often appeal to Seth for help as a clerk, as was the case that day. He was attending to one of the other young men in the valley who had come in for a few dry goods for his family, and the talk had naturally turned towards the threat of war. As soon as the word had been spoken, every other young male between the ages of sixteen and thirty had swarmed about the counter like flies around a jar of honey set out in the sun. Talk of war was more contagious than a yawn, and each day that passed only increased its effect on the men in the Chesson valley.

There was a total of about five boys from the surrounding farms gathered about Seth, William and James Taylor being among them. Fire leapt between their eyes and eagerness oozed from their mannerisms and attitudes. Not about to let someone beat his passion for the Confederacy, James countered, "Well, I've already got it all worked out. I've bought ole June from Pa, and I'm a'joinin' the cavalry as soon as I hear tell of where a regiment is forming."

Peter entered the General Store on the tail end of James' statement and the words snapped his head towards the speaker. So it was true.... Henry had told him this past Sunday that James was preparing to join the army when volunteers were called for, but Peter had resigned the statement to nothing more than a boyish interpretation of a conversation he had overheard. Yet now he had heard it from the young man himself. He started to greet James, but noticed Seth watching him warily and decided to simply get the nails he had come for.

He nodded in acknowledgement of the group which the various members returned with diverse levels of friendliness. While he searched for the intended items of purchase, he heard Seth continue, "I don't doubt your plans to join the war efforts, or any of you all for that matter. We have got to protect our rights, and I know you fellows will answer the call when it comes. But there are some—" his eyes shot towards Peter then back again "—whom may not be so inclined. They still think we are a part of the Union and desire to see our way of life changed. If you ask me, I would say they want to do away with Southern Society all together; they would like nothing better than to see our whole culture destroyed and the South become industrialized with all the corruption that comes with bigger cities. They're a shame to society. That's why those like ourselves must be all the more active in defending this land if it comes to it."

The other young men still gathered about the counter added their passionate agreement to Seth's words, completely unaware of whom the clerk intended them for. But Peter knew. Seth had never been a close friend of his, there was always something about the fellow that caused Peter to distrust him. But recently—especially since the day he and William delivered the news about Virginia's secession—Peter found Seth watching him closer and trying to act as a close comrade. Somedays he would simply drop by the farm with no apparent reason for being there. And while he conversed with Peter, his eyes never seemed to rest, searching for some sign that would throw a tarnish on Peter's name in the community. Other times, such as at the Sabbath meetings, Peter could feel Seth's eyes drilling holes in the back of his head, as if staring long enough would somehow reveal secrets that his mouth would not disclose.

Having weighed out the amount of nails he needed, Peter placed the sack on the counter in front of Seth. "Five pounds of eight's," he announced the quantity of his selection. Seth merely nodded, but placed the bag on his own scale and watched the needle come to rest at the five pound mark. He replaced the bag on the counter and commented with a smile that attempted to be reassuring, "Sorry about that, Pete. But with the way things are going in this day in time, you can never be too careful. You got a special project or something planned?"

"No...nothing out of my ordinary woodwork for those who hire me," Peter replied slowly, unsure of any hidden meaning that might have accompanied Seth's words. *Why did he want to know what I use them for?* The nails were to replenish his supply he had spent the previous week in helping replace a few shingles on the Taylor's old cabin that had blown off in a recent storm, the same building they hid runaways in. Peter wasn't sure what Seth might know, or if he knew anything at all, but he determined to stay more alert in his activities. "I was just running low on my supply and I had time this afternoon to come and in get some more."

Seth shrugged, "Just trying to be neighborly, z'all." What are you planning to do?"

"I beg your pardon?"

"About the war, blockhead. It's what we've been talking about in here for the past fifteen minutes. Which branch of the military are you planning to join?" When Peter did not immediately reply, Seth continued, "You are planning on joining the army, right?"

Peter remained steadfast under his steely gaze. With determination in his voice he answered, "I do not feel that the Lord is calling upon me to join any army – North or South. He takes no pleasure in the death of the wicked, so why should I, His mere servant, take pleasure in something He does not? And on top of that: there is no army to enlist with. So no, I do not plan on enlisting in any branch of service unless the Lord should direct my heart to do so."

"But what about your duty to Virginia," protested James. "I know you and Pa were against secession...but it's happened, and you can't do anything about that. The Confederacy is whom your loyalty should rest upon."

A smug grin played on Seth's face framed by a stubble of an attempt at growing a beard, his eyes seconding the question. Peter started to turn away, but caught himself and straightened his shoulders. "James, the Lord said, 'Sufficient for the day is its own trouble.' I will continue in what God has given me to do now; there is no Confederate army, so it does me no good to lay down plans for something that does not yet exist. But I will be praying...and I hope you all would join me in that." He set his jaw firmly, nodded his head, and strode through the store's front entrance.

The other young men followed him with their eyes, some full of consternation, some sympathy—and some filled with anger. Dropping his voice from its usual volume, Seth tried to appear ambiguous as he toyed with a loose strand of the roll of packing string and inquired, "Perhaps it is just me, but have any of you fella's noticed Peter acting mighty curious lately?"

"Well, I've always considered him a strange boy," one of his audience admitted.

"I give you that. But I am talking even more so. William—you two used to be close companions. It was a regular occurrence for you to tell me at meetings on Sundays of something you and Peter had done that week. When was the last time he has asked you to help him on a project?"

William remained silent, but Seth noticed the doubt beginning to creep into his eyes and pounced on it. "When was the last time he has simply come to spend an evening with your family? When was the last time your brother Henry went over and spent Saturday with him? James, am I wrong in asking these questions?"

"No, you're absolutely right," James affirmed. "That's been something I've noticed, and even little Henry has commented on how much he misses spending time with him. I know Peter has some things he is trying to work through right now, and perhaps he feels that it is better to focus on them. He does come over some to spend the evening meal with us, but it is not quite as frequent as it used to be. Still, I do not understand his withdraw from nearly everyone else around him."

"Exactly!" Seth triumphed in the concession. "I am not one to spread rumors or to try and defame another, but I have to ask, what is he hiding?"

"What do you think he is hiding?"

"I am not sure, but it might be anything. He may be a Unionist, and may even be thinking of going over to the North's side."

"Oh, come on now," William objected, his loyalty rising up in defense of the accusation leveled at his friend. "I do not know for certain the reason behind Peter's hesitation to want to join the army, but I have never heard him mention anything that would make me suspect he would desire to fight for the Union. He's one of the most honest young men I know, and he wouldn't keep something like that from me."

James began chewing his lower lip, then corrected his younger brother. "He might."

"No way."

"So you mean you do not remember how long he kept the fact from us that he had only come to Chesson after he had left his family's plantation?"

That remark restrained the quick response forming in William's mind.

"Wha…Peter on a plantation?" one of the other boys asked, disbelief filling his voice. "I thought he had just wanted to strike out on his own and had come to work for Samuel Kouffers."

"Well, that was part of it, but it only came about after his father basically told him to choose between his convictions about slavery or the family. After fourteen months, he said that—"

"He told us," William interjected hurriedly, "that it was a private matter. He never lied about any of it; he only did not feel it needed to be known publicly."

The revelation, however brief, was news to the rest of the young men, but the clerk used James' story to drive his point home. "I don't think any of us knew that—which is precisely my point. If he kept something like that back from some of his closest friends, would he not much more keep something like planning to join the Union secret?" He shook his head in wonder. "All I am saying is that I for one am going to be watching him closely—for we may have a traitor living here in Chesson."

■■

Drawing in a deep, level breath, Peter lowered his Springfield rifle, aiming at the small target he had placed in the yard, his finger resting snuggly against the trigger. Letting his breath out slowly, he squeezed and the rifle's hammer dropped. As the smoke cleared, he nodded with satisfaction at the toppled block of wood that had served as his target, laying on the ground beside the others he had previously struck.

Resting the butt of the gun on the ground, Peter measured out another round of powder. He hadn't practiced his shooting outside of hunting much before his work with the Underground, but at Charles' encouragement, he began to practice shooting on a more regular basis. Charles and William had insisted that it might be a matter of life or death, and though Peter hated to think he might have to make that choice, he practiced.

As he had begun to do so, he had discovered that practice shooting gave him a way to vent his frustration and anger that often wound up inside of him. The issues concerning the Confederacy and the possibility of an impending war often weighed heavy upon his spirit, and he despised those who treated it lightly, like Seth had done that morning in town. He had been wrestling with whether he would join the army or not, but as he had told Seth earlier, there was no military to join. He would wait on the Lord to guide him if war actually did occur.

He drove the ramrod home and raised the rifle to his shoulder, preparing to draw a bead on the final target when a voice arrested his attention. "What you been a'shooting, Peter?"

He started, then turned to face William striding across his yard toward him. He glanced back towards the targets, then returned to face his friend and shrugged. "I was just trying to get in a little target practice this afternoon, but that is all. How are you?"

William took his extended hand. "Tolerable, I'd say." Inspecting the targets beyond Peter, he commented, "You been out here long?"

"Not too long. I have not been shooting in a while, but I try to work in a few minutes every other week or so."

William nodded. "I see. Have you always done that, or is that something you started recently?"

"Oh, I suppose it has only been in the past few months," Peter shifted slightly. "Your father suggested that I do it, and with what you had said about the need to defend ourselves, I thought it would be wise...well, you know why."

"I think I do, but after this morning, I'm not so sure anymore."

"This morning? You mean with Seth at the store? I was just saying that I was not planning on joining the Confederacy, and that it was a mute issue, since there is no army to join."

"Is it because you are planning to go north?"

"What? Where did you hear that?"

"So it's true," William sighed dejectedly, his shoulders sagging.

"No, of course not!" Peter returned. "I am not planning on joining any army. Who told you that I was?" A shadow began to form upon his countenance. "Was it Seth?"

"Well, he did not actually say that you were, but he thought you might be. He thought with your views and how you have been acting recently and all, that maybe you were considering going up to Maryland or Pennsylvania or something."

"William, you're not making any sense. I am aware that many people know that I was opposed to secession, and some know how I view slavery. But what have I done that would cause someone to think I would be joining the Union now?"

"It is not exactly something that you have done, but more of what you have not done. You have been becoming more reclusive, distancing yourself from others, and," William sighed, running his fingers through his hair, "not telling the full truth."

"I can't go revealing to people what I do with the Underground—"

"That's not what I meant. I was thinking about your past."

The two men stared at each other, neither sure of what to say next, or even who should respond to the subject William had broached. Peter had the vague inclination again that his loyalty was being called into question.

Peter began slowly, "Will, I apologize once again for not having been forthright with you, but I had wanted to remove myself as far away from it as I could."

"And not telling us for fourteen months? And when you did tell us, you didn't tell me directly; you had Pa do it."

"Will, as I said, I apologize for keeping it from you. I should have come to each of you directly, but I was afraid. I told you that, and to tell the truth, I thought we had reached an understanding about it, putting the matter behind us."

"You're right," William sighed. "I am sorry for bringing it up again. We had dealt with it, you asked for forgiveness, and we gave it. It was just that with what Seth was saying, and James brought it up again—"

"Why did James say anything about it? Were you all talking about plantations, or slave holders?"

"No, we were talking about you. Seth was going on about you possibly keeping your decisions from us, and I tried to defend you, but Seth heard all he needed to."

"James said that I had been raised on a plantation, that I left, and that I had kept back that information in front of Seth and those other young men?"

"He did. I wish he hadn't of. It did not need to be said, not there."

Peter chewed his lip, anger flickering in his eyes, though not at the young man facing him. "That was not his to tell, and definitely not to Seth!" He shook his head, a deep sigh rising from within his chest. "Thank you for trying to defend me."

"I was not able to do much," William explained sheepishly. "Anyway, when I heard James and Seth talking about how secret you were, and Seth going on about you possibly going to the Union, I wanted to come hear the truth from you. I don't want things being said about you that are not true, or that you do not want being said."

"I appreciate that. Deeply. I give you my word: I will be perfectly honest with you."

"I believe you." He clapped a hand on his shoulder. "So, you are not planning on joining the Union then?"

"No, I am not. If it should come to war, I do not know what the Lord may lead me to do. He may call me to stay here, carry on the work of the Underground. He may lead me to defend the Union and try to reconcile the North and South, in a small way as I can. Or He may yet lead me to defend Virginia. I cannot tell now what He will lead me to do."

"But war is coming, Peter. We have to be ready. I don't want to fight against you, believe me, I don't."

"Why would you fight against me? We are friends, we both serve the Lord, we believe the slaves should be free, and we are each working towards that end. What are you talking about?"

"If you join the Union," William drilled with his eyes, pain filling them, "you will become my enemy. As soon as the call comes, I am going with Seth to join the Confederacy."

CHAPTER ELEVEN

Slowly watching the falling liquid with a weary eye, Peter poured another mug of coffee he had warmed over the fire, emptying the remainder of the percolator. Another group of runaways had come to the Taylor's the previous day, and Peter had spent the night leading the escaping slaves to the next station. After a few hours of sleep, Peter forced himself awake and worked most of the morning and the entire afternoon with Samuel. Fortunately, they were engaged in only a few simple jobs that demanded less concentration than other recent ones, but even still, Peter struggled to stay focused upon his task.

He sank into the chair, sipping the steaming liquid. He was often accused of drinking his coffee too hot, but he didn't care, not that evening. He had built up a tolerance to it, and his exhaustion superseded the protest of his tongue.

He still could not believe William's decision. Of course, he knew his friend was being swept up in the fervor of James and other men—had been for a long time—but even still, he never thought he would actually join the Confederate army, not with his efforts in the Underground.

William had explained that slavery was something to deal with regardless of whether their government was in Washington or Richmond, and since the war wasn't even about slavery, he could still do both—join the army while still supporting his family's secret work. He was fighting to bring the political power to the states, to keep it out of the bureaucrats already in power. As soon as it was all over, he said he would be right there again, helping the slaves to freedom alongside his family.

Peter cast an eye to the small cabinet he kept his food in, dreading the task that lay before him. Supper sounded quite appealing, but the idea of having to prepare it was protested by his weary body.

He took another sip of his coffee. It wasn't just the midnight run that was the cause of his weariness—it was the Confederacy. Volunteers for the state militia had been forming since Virginia had seceded from the Union, with more and more young men flocking to pledge themselves to their homeland's defense. It had only taken a few weeks for Seth to enlist, which decision had only been followed by James a few days later, and William after that. It was not an army for the Confederacy as of yet per se, but the talk was that it would not be much longer before those battalions would become regiments of the Confederate army of Northern Virginia.

As more and more of the young men of the Chesson valley enlisted, Peter felt his own loyalty being scrutinized even further. Though a few other young men about his own age had yet to sign their names to a regiment, Peter knew he was a part of a marked minority—a minority that found the number of its members shrinking with each passing week. He feared it would not be much longer before he would find himself the only unmarried young man in the entire valley who had not chosen to take up arms for Virginia. It was not being the outsider that concerned him. What he feared was what that fact might do to his reputation...and to his relationship with his neighbors.

He was not a vain man. If his reputation became tarnished and he was cast off as a Unionist to be despised, he would submit to that label. Yet when he considered what might happen if the suspicion he was under increased, what might be revealed. His unusual habit of coming to work late after conducting a group of runaways was largely unknown in the valley, and aside from a few odd individuals, no one seemed to pay his routines any mind. But if suspicions rose and he began to be studied, the odd patterns of his travels might provoke further scrutiny. He was not willing to risk what that examination might reveal, not with the Taylors and their own work in the Underground.

The knock on his cabin door pulled Peter from the enticing slumber he had begun to succumb to. Rising from his chair and setting his half-emptied mug upon the table, he stepped to the door and lifted the latch.

Henry stood before him, cap cocked in its usual disheveled manner to one side, a smile upon his little face. "Evening, Peter," he greeted gaily.

"Evening, Henry," Peter returned, though at a less energetic manner. "How are you?"

"Fine, thank you. How 'bout yourself?"

"I am well, thank you very much."

Henry stared up at him, studying his face, his curiosity stirring with in him. "You look mighty tired. What you been a doin'?"

"Well, I am a little tired, I admit. I have just been busy with a few projects that I could put off no longer and required my attention. I'll be fine after tonight, though."

"That's what I came over fer, about tonight I mean."

"Oh, is that so?" Peter returned, not even bothering to correct his young neighbor's speech.

"Yes sir. Ma said that we's got plenty of food on, and says for me to see if you be a'willing to come for supper. Will ya come?"

Peter weighed his options in his mind, considering the value of each. He had planned on cooking the last of the ham he had, then going straight to bed, getting the sleep he had denied his body the previous evening. Yet he considered how many times over the past several months he had refused the offers of his neighbors. With one last glance in his cabin, Peter took his own hat off its rack and pulled the door behind him. "I would be pleased to join your family for supper tonight."

"Thank you, Peter! It's been ages since you've come," Henry rejoiced.

As the two turned their steps onto the lane leading between the two cabins, Henry continued his exuberant speech. "Things have been harder with William and James off drilling away in the army. George has been taking care more of the farm work, and Robert too. That just leaves me and Emily, and girls ain't no fun."

"Oh, they are not, are they?"

"They do nothing! All they like is to play with little dolls. Emily won't go down to the creek with me, she don't like to play war, and—"

Peter gripped Henry's shoulder, halting their tread. An intense expression set deep in his eyes, he squatted so as to look the boy full in the face. With a measured tone full of suppressed emotion, Peter rebuked him. "Henry, war is not something we should rejoice about. Wars consist of battles, and battles are only made by men killing one another, by one man shedding the blood of another human created in the image of God. There is nothing glorious about war, nothing we should celebrate. Please, do not think that it is a game that grown men play. Nothing could be farther from the truth." He sighed. "Do you understand what I am saying?"

Although with a look that revealed doubt behind his words, Henry nodded slowly. "Yes."

"I know William and James have talked so much about joining the military, and they make it sound fun, but do not think that. It is not." Peter patted the boy's shoulder, then rose to his full height. "And if the Lord wills, hopefully this will all end before we truly come to the point of war."

Silence reigned between the two as they walked. Henry's words only cemented Peter's evaluation of the flippant attitudes of many of the young men who had enlisted. Their manner, tone, and words had stirred the concept that war was a glorious thing, as if it was honorable for one man to kill another. The view angered Peter incessantly, a fact revealed by the intense lines carved upon his forehead as he walked with Henry to the boy's home.

On his part, Henry did not know what to make of Peter's abrupt interruption. He knew his friend did not share his own brother's opinion of the Confederacy, but he saw little in their situation that had caused such strong conviction in Peter.

Kicking a loose stone with the toe of his slightly-oversized boot, Henry finally ventured, "Peter?"

"Yes, Henry?"

"Why do you hate war so much? James said there wouldn't be much killin'. He said there'd be some shooting, people would get scared, and then everything would be over. Isn't that what will happen?"

"I pray it is, Henry. But I do not know if your brother is right. The reasons we may be at war have been going on for so long, I do not think they will dissolve in one single engagement of the two forces.

No, Henry, I fear this will be much longer than what James or William have told you."

He glanced down at his young companion. Checking the gloom that had begun to creep into his voice, Peter straightened Henry's cap. "Now, don't you be worrying about it. Maybe James is right, maybe this will be over here shortly. At any rate, you just keep your mind on your work…and on your books."

"Aw, not you too," Henry wined, though his mood began to brighten from the somberness a moment before. "Ma was already onto me about that."

"It's good for a boy to be kept in line by his mother. Mine had to do a work on me, I tell you."

He turned in at the parted gate, Henry following right on his heels. Out of habit, he glanced towards the clothes line. A few items hung there, but the signal quilt he searched for was absent from among them. Turning back to Henry, he remarked, "I wonder what Shawna's got on for supper this evening."

"I think I's hear her tell Ma that she was a working up a beef stew or something."

Peter playfully pulled the boy's cap low over his eyes. "Jenny's still got a ways to go with teaching you how to talk, doesn't she?"

"I'ls learn one day," Henry laughed. Then all of a sudden, "Thank you, Peter."

"Thank you? For what?"

"For being like you used to be. I miss coming over and watching you work, or even you messing with me like you did just now. I like it."

The boy's words stabbed Peter's conscience. He knew he had been neglecting him for a while now, especially since he had begun work on the Underground. Though he had determined many times to restore their friendship, he had not made a diligent effort to preserve their relationship as they had known it previously. But staring down into Henry's eyes, Peter knew he had to do more.

"I'm sorry, Henry. I have missed our times together as well. There have been a few issues that have arisen this year that I have become preoccupied with, and I have not been a good friend to you. I cannot spend quite as much time with you as we used to before things changed, but I will make a better effort in finding time to be with you. I know that things are difficult with James and William gone, so maybe I should start helping your father and George out here on the farm some more."

They had reached the door, and after rapping his knuckles upon the oak boards, Peter pushed the door open. As they stepped inside, the sounds of Shawna ordering the final stages of supper preparations from the kitchen greeted their ears. Peter smiled. Shawna was one of those women who had the odd mixture of a gruff exterior combined with a heart of gold, and though she often sounded harsh, her love for her family and the Taylors was stronger than any Peter had ever seen.

Emily was just laying the last utensils upon the table, and as Peter closed the door behind them, she bounded to his side. "Evenin', Peter."

"Evening. And how are you?"

"Fine. Did you see?"

"See what?" Peter chuckled softly at her enthusiasm.

"See me set the table myself," Emily reported, swelling with pride at her accomplishment.

Peter surveyed the table, then gazed down at the girl. "I'm afraid I did not see you actually set it, but it looks mighty fine."

"Thank you, Peter," she smiled at his praise.

"She's been waiting to show you for so long," Jenny commented, laying aside her sewing and rising from a chair in the room to the side of the dining area. "Loressa had been working with her and working with her, and she had finally got it. And then, just a few weeks ago, Loressa had turned the task over to her." She stepped to her sister's side and affectionately stroked the auburn curls.

Glancing up at Peter, she continued, "I take it then that you are joining us for supper?"

"Yes. Henry asked me, and to be honest, I certainly did not feel like making anything myself."

She smiled softly, understanding the hidden reference to their work. Glancing behind her to find Henry occupied with Robert in bringing in more wood through the back door, she patted her sister's head. "Emily, how about you go see if Loressa needs any help getting anything else ready."

"Okay," she happily complied.

As the girl scampered off to the kitchen, Jenny turned back to face Peter. "I take it everything went alright last night?"

"Yeah. No problems. I know those woods well, but that full moon we had certainly helped."

"I'm glad. It seems that the time between each group is growing shorter and shorter."

"You are telling me," Peter sighed, though not from exasperation.

With concern creasing her forehead, Jenny inquired, "Are you alright? You seem quite tired."

Peter chuckled.

Confused by his response, Jenny inquired, "What? What's funny about that?"

"Oh, nothing. Henry just asked me that a little while ago. I'm tired, but I'll be fine. You are right, when I first started making those runs, sometimes weeks or even a month would go by between a group of runaways coming. Now it seems like they are coming every couple of days."

"I know. We have been cooking so much more. It's getting harder and harder to hide it from George. I think he knows we are doing something, but I do not know if he knows exactly what it is."

"I was wondering if you all had told him, with James and William being gone more."

She shook her head gently. "No, not yet. I think father will tell him soon, though."

"I know he will do it when he believes it is best. Speaking of your brothers, have you all heard from James or William lately?"

"No, not really," her face fell. "Last we heard, they were doing well and excited to actually be joining the Confederate army, whenever that will happen."

"From what I have heard, it won't be too long. It seems that there is talk of it happening before the end of next month."

"That soon?"

"I'm afraid so. But," he forced a smile, "as I was telling Henry, maybe this will end before long and our Nation will be reconciled to itself and tensions can begin to heal."

"I hope you are right," she sighed. "I hate to think what might happen if war does erupt."

CHAPTER TWELVE

Peter laid the paper back upon his table and took another bite of his biscuit, wiping his hands upon his pants. He glanced out the window, dingy from a lack of washing, observing the setting sun. Some time still remained before he would have to lead another group of runaways at the Taylor's.

Picking up the sheets again, he glance down at the letter from Olivia. Nearly two months had passed since her last letter, and he had stopped by the post office that afternoon before returning from work.

She had been bemoaning the fact that fewer balls had been hosted in her area, since it limited the opportunities Lawrence had to take her out. Peter sighed, shaking his head. The fellow was still pursuing her, even with all that their country and state were facing.

On a more positive note, she wrote that their family was in good health. His father occupied himself with the political situation and the plantation, carrying on in his normal fashion. Their mother was taking the recent events quite well, she had said, and had sent her love.

Peter sighed and replaced the letter once again, leaning back in his chair. In all of her letters since he had left home, Olivia had never mentioned anything about her father in reference to Peter, either good or bad. He had no inkling of whether his father still regarded him as betraying the family's heritage, or whether he was beginning to forgive him. The information he longed for had also been absent from his mother's letters as well. Still, he was thankful for what they did choose to include in their letters.

Pushing himself away from the table, Peter rose and stepped to the small cabinet in the corner. Though he predominately kept his flour and meal in it, he also had placed the few sheets of writing paper and pencils he possessed. Taking the stack of pages and one of the stub pencils, he returned to his seat and prepared his reply. *Dearest Olivia,* he wrote.

Footsteps upon the stairs outside directed his attention away from his writing, and he turned in anticipation of the knock he knew was imminent. He rose as it sounded and strode to the door.

The opening door revealed Henry standing in the light of the slowly sinking sun, an eager smile of expectation upon his face. "Hello, Henry," Peter smiled down at his visitor. "How are you?"

"Doin' fine, thank you. Ma didn't have anything 'round the house fer me to do, so I reckoned I'd come over here and see what you were up to."

"Is that so? I did not have much going on, just writing a reply to a letter I received from my sister," he pointed over his shoulder into the cabin behind him.

"Oh, that's boring stuff," Henry rolled his eyes. "Ya got a cabinet or something yer building?"

"Not real—" then remembering his earlier determination, "—actually, I do believe I have a project we could work on. I had been putting it off, but I suppose we could work on it now, start it at least."

He took his coat off its rack and stepped onto the porch, pulling the cabin's door closed after him. The pair strolled across the yard towards the barn, and once inside, Peter retrieved an oak board nearly the length of his forearm and laid it upon the work bench. As Peter struck a match in an old lantern he kept suspended from a rafter, Henry pulled himself to his perch upon the top of the work table.

Repositioning his cap, the boy inquired, "What you makin' with this?"

"Well," Peter replied, retrieving various chisels, "Mr. Kouffers has been attempting to teach me how to carve a design onto a panel for cabinet doors, but I am very slow at the task. I figured I could use some of these old boards and practice here on my own." He pulled out the pencil he had deposited in his pocket and began to sketch a large design comprised of shapes and letters upon the board.

Tilting his head in absorbed interest, Henry quarried, "Why ya putting a 'W' on it?"

"This is the design of the Wilson family crest. We have just completed their cabinet at the shop, and I remembered the design distinctly, and since it is fairly intricate, I figured it would be a good one to practice with." He reached for a mallet and the largest chisel he had laid upon the bench.

Describing the process of each step of the work, Peter struck the tool with the mallet, roughing out the sketch, giving the design depth. With each successively smaller chisel size, Henry watched with rapt attention as the design Peter had drawn took shape and grew deeper into the board's surface. With only the finest details remaining, Peter laid aside his mallet, applying pressure upon the chisel with his mere hands, controlling with acute precision each stroke he made upon the wood's grain.

Laying the chisel back alongside its companions upon the table, Peter blew the small shavings and wood particles from the board and admired his work. Though not nearly cut with the same craftmanship Samuel possessed, he decided it was a closer resemblance to the design than his previous attempts. His employer had reminded him that the skills of their trade took time, precious time to master. Peter was patient, though, and he did not allow his small progress to discourage him.

He shifted the board so Henry could gaze at it more fully. "What do you think?"

Henry rubbed his hands along the surface of the crest carved into the deep grain of the oak. "It is a fine job, Peter. It looks mighty good."

"Thank you. If you think this one is good, you should see Mr. Kouffers'. They are positively beautiful."

Henry raised his head towards Peter. "Do you think you could teach me how to carve?"

"Well now, it is not easy—"

"Oh, but please!" he begged. "Just something small."

Peter met the imploring gaze of his young friend. As he remembered his own early attempts at carving, an idea struck him. "I suppose we could give it a try. Do you have your pocket knife with you?"

"I have it right here," Henry shoved his hand inside his knickers, producing the tool, as Peter strode to the opposite side of the barn and bent down to retrieve a few small blocks of wood.

"Now to begin," Peter returned and placed himself beside Henry upon the table, "you hold the block of wood in your hand like so, see? Then, let me see your knife, then we need to figure out what we are going to make...."

In a fashion similar to how he accompanied his earlier techniques with his words, Peter narrated how to choose a design, how to properly make strokes with the knife's blade, and how to work with each of the different wood types. After describing a particular point, he would hand the block and knife to his companion, watching Henry's attempts to mimic the process just shown him. As needed, Peter offered helpful correction, demonstrating an easier or safer way to produce the same desired result.

"And so, we push it like this, keeping enough room for the duck's head." Peter glanced out the barn doors at the fading light. Setting the half-finished wooden duck beside him, he folded the boy's knife and returned it to Henry. "It is getting late, and I don't want your mother to be worrying about you. You had probably best be getting on home."

"Oh, but couldn't we work a little longer? You almost have all of his bill finished."

"No, not tonight. Tell you what, though—you keep this," he slid the carving towards him, "and work on it over the next couple of days. If you bring it back over on Saturday, I can show you how to continue shaping the body, sound good?"

"Thank you, Peter." Henry smiled warmly, taking up the wooden block in his hand and jumping to the barn's floor.

"You're welcome," Peter matched his action, following him to the barn's entrance. "Don't waste any time on your way back now, hear? That sun's going down fast."

"I won't, I promise. Thank you again, Peter."

"You're welcome. I enjoyed it. Give my greetings to your family."

"I will."

Peter watched his retreating figure until it disappeared around a bend, then turned his own steps towards his cabin. It had been some time since he had practiced his carving of small wooden figures, but the skill was not so lost that he could not instruct Henry on the basics. If he would devote a few minutes each day to resurrecting his former ability, he knew it would be an activity Henry and himself would enjoy working on together.

After retrieving his rifle and accouterments, he shut his cabin up behind him and started for the woods. He had only made the run a few nights previously, but with William having left to enlist, the full weight of conductor for the runaways had fallen upon his shoulders. Though he often drug himself through the day following a night-expedition, he took to the work with a willing heart, grateful that the Lord had allowed him to be a part of it, to carry on the work while William was away.

Moving as noiselessly as he could through the underbrush, Peter slipped through the forest, skirting around the Taylor's fields until he came to the old shed upon the low hill. Drawing up near the door, he rapped three times in quick succession, then slipped inside the structure. Without waiting to locate those now in his charge, he whispered, "Hello, my name is Peter Brenton. I am your guide tonight."

Three sets of eyes peered back at him from the far corner as a voice called in a thick, heavy accent, "My name's Gabriel, and dis is my son Stephen, and his wife, Mollie."

"Alright," Peter nodded. "I am a friend of the Taylors, and I have made this journey many times before. There is not much of a moon out tonight, so when we go, stay close by me. Do not fear, the Lord will be with us, and I pledge to you that I will give my life to see you safely through. Are you ready?"

"Yes sar," returned Gabriel, solemn determination in his voice.

"Very well then." Peter opened the rear door of the cabin. "Let us go."

As the three Negros slipped past him, Peter indicated with his rifle's barrel the direction they were to head, then followed after he closed the door softly behind them. Switching his rifle to his left hand, Peter over took them, gliding into the lead position and plunged into the greater darkness of the forest. A delicate balance lay between haste and reckless noise that would be the tell-tale sign of a group of fleeing fugitives. Peter also knew he had to pace himself and those following for the journey, for it would take the greater part of the night. Yet he knew those in his charge would give their all to reach freedom, and he would give them his all to help them reach their goal.

A snapping of a branch off ahead of him to the right sent Peter's blood racing and he felt his stomach tighten. Instinctively, he raised his hand to motion the runaways to the ground, but they had prostrated themselves the moment the sound broke upon their ears. Peter pressed himself against a large Gum, using the trunk as a shield between himself and the direction of the noise. Muffling the sound with his shirt, Peter gently eased the hammer of his rifle into position, then pivoted till he could just see around the tree.

Emptiness met his eyes. Warily, he scanned the surrounding woods for any sign of what lay before them, his search revealing nothing. No matter how many times he heard noises in the woods, he always felt himself grow tense as his imagination played upon his fears, both on behalf of himself and those he led.

Peter was about to give the signal to move on when the sound came again, and this time, his sharp eye caught the motion of a low bush thirty yards beyond the cowering fugitives. With a deep inhale of breath, he slowly raised the rifle to his shoulder, resting his finger upon the trigger, then waited.

The branches of the bush parted and a young doe emerged, leading her fawn behind her. Peter let out a low sigh of relief as his hand relaxed. Reversing his earlier action, he brought the hammer to rest upon the firing nipple and motioned the three runaways to rise. "It was only a doe," he hissed. "Always better to be cautious."

Stepping back onto the trail, he started along their previous path, the runaways close at his heels. No, he told himself, he could not risk it. Though he might feel foolish at having given the alarm for only a passing deer, one look at the implicit trust that appeared in the eyes of those in his charge confirmed his evaluation. He could not be too cautious, he decided. There was too much at stake.

CHAPTER THIRTEEN

The stars dispelled the darkness with the aid of the moon, their brilliance only slightly dimmed by the light radiating from the lanterns scattered throughout the town square. Dancers swung with their partners in the combined light of the night sky and the small flames while a band, set on a small wooden stage, played a lively melody. Folks from the surrounding farms mingled about the outside of the area separated for the dances, sharing with one another whatever news each had to give. Joy seemed to radiate from all faces, and above them all hung the Stars and Bars, The Bonnie Blue Flag.

There was nothing beautiful about it, Peter mused as he helped himself to another roll from the plates set upon the few tables to one side of the square. It was mid-June, and Virginia had passed the law that would send her volunteer militia to join the Confederate army already forming. It was the last night the volunteers from Chesson would be home before they left to fulfill their duty, and the valley had come together to send their men and boys off properly.

Pies, cakes, and cobblers had been baked in abundance. Breads and chicken had been provided for a group twice as large as actually had attended. And in the side alleys away from the women and children, a man might even help himself to a little whiskey, all in celebration of course.

The day had seemed so far off, but when it had arrived, Peter felt that his country was slipping even farther apart. Up to that point, the conflict had been local issues, their state only concerning itself with militias in case of invasion. But with the completion of the festivities that night, Virginia would officially join herself to the rest of the South militarily.

Returning to the post he had selected as his observation point, Peter absently chewed the last of the roll he had shoved in his mouth. He had on his Sunday best like everyone else, but merely because he had no other options for such an occasion—practically every other set of pants had either holes or stains from his work. He surveyed his neighbors from the surrounding farms. Though the gaiety of the event seemed nearly universal, Peter felt the absence of any pull to rejoice. Not with what weighed upon his spirit.

Jenny was just finishing a dance set with William, and as they applauded the band after the final notes, she curtsied to her brother and made her way towards the crowd, her eyes searching. She found him and made her way towards the pole he rested against. "I didn't know if you would come," she greeted him warmly, an encouraging smile upon her face.

Peter straightened and tried to return her smile as she approached. "I thought about it, and I decided it was the right thing for me to do."

"I'm glad you came, there is so much food here. Shawna seemed to think that she had to cook for the whole Chesson valley," Jenny laughed.

"Oh, I can just hear her now," Peter chuckled, though his laugh was not his warm, hearty one.

Jenny studied him for a moment. "Well," she sighed determinedly, a sparkle in her eye, "you look like you could use some cheering up. It's not good for you to be always gloomy the way you are these days. Would you like to dance? If you asked for the next one, I would accept."

Peter glanced at his young neighbor. Her hair was pulled back in its usual bun, though a few strands had struggled loose due to her recent activity. The dress she was wearing was a simple, pale blue that she often wore for meetings, accented by the smile in her eyes. His sister Olivia used to smile with her eyes like that, he remembered. He hadn't seen her in so long...

Almost as though he regretted his answer, Peter shook his head. "No, I'm afraid I don't dance. My tutor taught me and Olivia growing up, but that was years ago. Well, I should say he taught Olivia, he tried to teach me, but I never caught on. I have never been good at it, and I'm afraid I'll make a poor partner tonight."

Her smile began to fade slightly. "You are thinking about what happens after tonight, aren't you?"

He solemnly nodded. "I am. I only came tonight to show myself a friend to William, and to James. That, and to show that I am still a part of this community. I did not come to have a good time. If it was not for your family, with your brothers going off and your father's views on certain matters, I probably would not have even come."

"I know," she sighed. "When I think about that, sorrow fills my heart. I don't want William or James to go. But I try to think of what they are going to remember from tonight, their last time being with us for who knows how long, only God knows. I think of what it might do to them if the last memory they have is one of gloom and strife with their family. It is for their sake that I'm trying to have a good time, trying not to think about what lies ahead."

Peter bit his lower lip, his eyes drifting towards the dancers swinging together in pairs along the line of the dance. Was Jenny right considering how their actions might affect William and James? He was not entirely sure how his own actions towards her might affect William, but maybe he should put forth the effort to enjoy himself. For William's sake, anyway.

Turning his attention back towards Jenny, Peter smiled. "I believe you are right. I suppose I am not giving William a fond memory of his last night by acting like I am." He straightened, a teasing smile toying with his lip. "Miss Taylor, may I have that next dance?"

"You may, Mr. Brenton," She giggled, curtsying gently. As she released her skirt, she laughed, "Peter, I haven't heard you talk like that in ages."

"I suppose it has been some time," he chuckled in agreement.

"Oh, and speaking of fond memories," she continued, "Henry has really appreciated you letting him come over a little more. He especially enjoyed what you have been showing him with carving; he spends every spare minute working on those blocks you gave him.   I know it's not like it used to be between you two, but it means so much to him. It was so strange, the way you had withdrawn from him, from William, from all of us really." She studied him curiously. "What happened, Peter? What changed?"

Stealing a glance towards those who stood closest, Peter lowered his voice, "I apologize for my odd withdrawal. I did not mean to cause issues like I have done, but I did it to protect your family."

"To protect us?"

"Yes. When I started…helping your father with moving valuables, I did not think much about my relationship to your family. But as states began to secede and I did not meet the fervor and passion of other young men in the area, I realized that I might be bringing undo suspicion on your family by my close association with you all. Your father is known for not fully embracing the Confederacy, as I am. Your father is known to oppose slavery, as am I. If things continued as they have, your family and I will be two pockets of resistance to the new national spirit. I am still fairly new to the valley, though your family has long been respected here. Your two older brothers are going to fight for the Confederacy, while I remain behind. I am already being suspected of being a Northern sympathizer, and not wishing any investigation to reveal...you know what, I began to distance myself. I am not sure if I am making sense, but I did it to try and dispel as much association between myself and your family, for your all's sake and for your father's work."

Jenny nodded in understanding. "I see. I appreciate that, as I am sure my parents do. Do they know the reason why?"

"I have told them that I wanted to avoid making any obvious connection between myself and your family with what we are engaged in, so yes, they know. That is why I have just been taking the...loads myself without coming to the house and why I have not come to supper with you all as I used to. I did not want my marred reputation to taint your family's."

"I do not think that it would, but I am grateful for your concern. We had a batch come through a few days ago—did you deliver them well?"

Peter nodded. "Yes, I did. We had to halt a few times, but it was just a deer. I do not take any chances, so that is why..." Peter noticed the dance set had stopped and saw Seth striding towards them. "So, work has been going well. Samuel has been finding enough work, and though we are not as busy as we have been before, we have a fair amount of sets lined up."

"Well," Seth cut in as he joined them, "I have been staying busy with my work, the work of defending my Nation. Peter, why don't you join us? They are taking new recruits every day, and we can use every man we can get. Come with us, stand by our side in defense of Virginia."

"My answer remains the same, Seth, and unless the Lord leads me otherwise, I cannot join you. You have made your choice, and I have made mine. Let us leave it at that for now."

"Fair enough." Seth turned towards Jenny. "Would you honor me by giving me the next dance?"

Casting a quick, sidelong glance towards Peter, she replied, "I would, but I am already engaged this set with Peter."

"With Peter? He's staying at home, afraid to do his duty when called upon. Come on, Jenny. Give this soldier a dance before he goes off to war like a loyal Virginian. Peter can wait."

"But, Seth, I have alr—"

"It's alright, Jenny," Peter interjected, avoiding Seth's triumphant gaze. "Remember what we said a moment ago. This is their last night. If they do another round, I will take the next set. Go on with Seth. I'll wait."

"Well, it's good to see you have some patriotism still in you, my boy," Seth snickered victoriously, giving his arm to Jenny. "Don't worry. I won't keep her long."

Casting a regretful glance over her shoulder, Jenny followed Seth to the new line of couples forming for the next dance. William passed them, making his way towards Peter side, his manner a model of the joy that pervaded the evening.

"Hey, ole boy. How are you enjoying yourself?"

"Well, thank you." He surveyed his friend. "You seem to be worn out from all of that dancing."

"I tell you, I cannot remember the last time I have danced so much," William laughed. "Oh, we have not had a gathering like this in years. Not with all of the neighbors and everyone coming in, that is." He slapped Peter on the shoulder. "Say, I don't think I've seen you dancing yet. Have you taken a turn out there this evening?"

"No, I haven't."

"Why? You opposed to dancing or something?"

"No, not really. I was going to dance this set with your sister, but Seth came and took her."

"Oh, Seth," William sighed exasperatedly, his eye finding the young man forming the line with Jenny. A twinkle formed in William's eye as he cast a sidelong glance at Peter. "Was there something more that I heard in your voice than mere annoyance with Mason?"

"I beg your pardon?"

"Is it just that Seth annoys you, or was it the fact that he is dancing with Jenny and you aren't?"

Understanding of William's meaning sparked in Peter's mind, his face flushing with slight embarrassment at the insinuation. "No, it's not what you think, William…"

"Is it not? You are a little sweet on her, aren't you?"

"No, not like that. I assure you that there is nothing between your sister and myself in that way. I do consider her a friend, but more as of a sister than anything else. You are my friend, and she is your sister, and there is nothing beyond that, I assure you."

"Oh, I am sure," William consented, though the tease did not leave his eye. "But just for the record, I would not be opposed to having you as a closer kind of brother, if you catch my drift. Not saying anything," he flung up his hands, "just putting it out there. Now, I'll leave it alone."

"I appreciate that. I think that the Lord will lead me to marry one day, but I do not know when, nor do I even have an idea of whom. Furthermore, with the state of our Nation right now, I do not deem it wise to think about those things at this moment. Maybe after things are settled, but right now there are too many issues that would prevent me from focusing upon it."

"I can understand that. But look on the bright side," he playfully punched Peter's shoulder. "We will all array ourselves against the Federals a few times, and in a couple of weeks, all this will be behind us and life will move on. Things will still be tense for a while, naturally, but they will work themselves out. Nothing really major is going to happen. It couldn't happen.

Even though we have separated, we are all still Americans. We are not going to go on killing one another over these issues. We just have to show a strong front, prove to the folks in Washington that we are serious about this, and they will leave us alone. That is all that there is to it. So don't be starting to get all gloomy on me again."

"You think that is all that there will be?"

"Of course, Peter! Sure, they may call it a war, but it is not going to be like we had in the revolution, or even with Mexico. You just watch—by the time we start getting ready for winter, all this will be past and they will be putting it in the history books."

The dance set was coming to an end, and as the applause faded at the tune's conclusion, a tall gentlemen in a fine, dapper suit stepped onto the platform, clutching a few sheets of paper in his right hand. With a resounding voice that carried across the crowd, the man began, "Good evening, ladies and gentlemen. It pleases me very much to see our community come together on this occasion to support one another and to take a stand as we perform our duty to Virginia." He raised his hand to quiet the swelling applause.

"I am sure we all know why we have gathered here tonight on this fine evening, and I am equally as persuaded that each and every one of you knows the significance of tonight. Virginia has always been our home, will always be our home. And now, that home is being threatened by those who seek to destroy it. The call has been sent forth, and Virginia has answered, this valley in particular has answered.

"And so tonight, as we send our men and boys off to defend our glorious state, we want to show them that they will be with us in our thoughts, our hearts, and our prayers until they return again victorious on a day not too distant from this evening. Chesson, let us give our soldiers of the Confederacy a hearty round of applause to show our admiration, love, and support."

The crowd exploded with the sounds of a couple hundred hands clapping while the band played *Dixie*. As the applause faded, the speaker continued, "Men who are leaving us tonight to fulfill their duty to Virginia, know that you are not going to fight for today, or even for the next day. You are fighting for your future, your children's future, your grandchildren's future. You are fighting for Virginia. Be strong, and may God bring all of you home very soon." Again, the crowd erupted with applause.

The music commenced again, and the folks who had gathered mingled with one another once more, exchanging parting farewells as all prepared to take their families home to their respective farms and houses. Peter lent his assistance to the Taylors as they loaded their wagon with the table and the remainder of the food that they had brought. Little Emily was nearly asleep as Peter lifted her up to her mother in the wagon. Mary was struggling with the emotion of the evening, trying desperately to conceal the fact. *Who could blame her?* Peter reflected. He offered an encouraging smile. "Good night, Mrs. Taylor."

"Good night," she forced a smile in return.

Peter took his leave of the rest of the Taylor family until only Charles, James, and William remained. With an outstretched hand, Peter stepped to Charles. "Good night, sir."

"Good night. Thank you for coming."

"You are welcome, sir. I know you came for the same reason I did."

Charles nodded solemnly. "I know it meant a lot to them. I may be calling upon you as you have time to help with some of the work on the farm, with the boys being gone now, if you would not mind."

"I would be honored, sir. I will help as often as you need. Good night."

He exchanged farewells with James and wished him Godspeed as he journeyed to join his regiment, assuring him of his prayers. James thanked him warmly, deeply grateful for the gesture. Peter nodded his head in acknowledgement, then turned to face William.

The two young men gripped each other's forearm, then embraced one another, Peter slapping William on the back. "I will be praying for you, my friend."

"And I will be for you, with your work with Pa and everything."

"Thank you. I pray that you are right about this conflict."

"I am," William smiled, climbing on to the back of the wagon. As Charles clicked the reigns and the wagon started forward, William nodded back towards Peter and called, "Harvest time, Pete. You'll see. We'll be home by the harvest."

CHAPTER FOURTEEN

With another stroke of the hoe, Peter pulled the soil over the barley seed laying in the loose soil, then paused to wipe the sweat beading on his brow underneath his wide-brimmed leather hat. The back of his shirt had soaked through hours ago, but that was a normal occurrence for a man working in the Virginian fields in the middle of July. It had been some weeks since Peter had agreed to assist in the farming needs on the Taylor farm, and with his work with Samuel Kouffers becoming more sporadic, Peter found himself working in his neighbor's fields regularly.

He had worried about what other families in the valley might say, but Peter had determined that working for the Taylors was different than merely passing a relaxing evening with them. Helping a family while their sons had left for the war was being a member of the community and a matter of business more than friendship, so Peter had laid aside his qualms and set about his work readily.

That day in the fields, he had been helping George since just after dawn prepare the ground and plant a stand of late barley. Charles had noted that he usually tried to get his grain in a few weeks earlier, but with everything that had happened, he had not been able to attend to it. Charles had to drive in to town that morning, and Peter had eagerly offered to help George who had remained behind to plant the crop.

Resuming his work, Peter glance towards the edge of the field. George had worked his way to the end and had turned and was laying seed as he made his way back to the opposite side of the field. They only lacked a few more rows before they would complete their task, and by a quick glance toward the sinking sun, Peter knew that the day light would not permit them to do much more than that.

"Do you think we have enough seed to finish up?" Peter called as he continued to drag the clods that lay beside furrows back over the seeds.

George peered into his sack, then continued to drop the barley into the row he walked alongside. "I reckon so. We ain't got but two or three more passes till we're finished, and I'd say that I have that at least left in here."

"That will be good."

"I'm telling you. I'm about ready to eat me some of that roast for supper then hit the bed." With William and James having left for the Confederacy, the brunt of the farm work they had previously performed fell on George's shoulders. Peter tried to help as often as he could, but George still felt the weight that his brother's absence left. Usually the quiet type, he was rarely heard to complain, thus when he did, it was evidence of great weariness and exhaustion.

"That sounds like a fine idea. I wish I could join you on that, but I have a few things that I must attend to this evening." The signal quilt had been hanging on the line when Peter had arrived at the Taylor's home that morning, but he did not know if George knew about the Underground work yet or not. "Though I do have to admit, I am looking forward to that roast myself."

"I've had a hankering for a roast for quite a spell, so I can hardly wait to sink my teeth into that meat tonight." He looked over and grinned at Peter. "And working like this will sure stir up a mighty fierce appetite, you know?"

"You are right there," Peter chuckled.

"Ma and Pa should be getting back right soon, I suspect."

"What did they have to get anyway?"

"Oh, normal things. Ma needed some dry goods, Jenny wanted to get some more cloth and thread, Pa wanted a few things himself. Course, Henry and Emily were just excited to get to go into town, and Robert, well, I'm not sure why he went, but he's with them anyhow."

"I don't make it over to that part of town very often, only riding out there when necessity compels me to. Do you have opportunity to make it out that way with your family often?"

"Not recently, not with James and Will being gone. Too many things 'round here on the farm that need attending to. I can't hardly find time to break way. And if things continue like they are, I won't be going back to school in the fall, neither. Someone has to work with

Pa, and I can't do that just when I'm home in the afternoons."

"You won't be going back to school? What will your sister or your mother say?"

George shrugged. "Ma knows work comes first. Jenny will just have to realize that as well. Besides, I would have graduated in another year or so as it was, and I don't figure that I'm going to be missing much from that. And even if I will, it doesn't matter. I have to work."

"So you don't think it will be over quickly like some folk say?"

"I ain't sure. I know Will said that this will pass, and folks like Mr. Jones agree with him, but I know Pa thinks this will take a lot longer. I just ain't sure."

"I am not sure either. I want to believe that William is right, but I fear that this conflict might drag on longer than anyone imagines." Peter pulled the last soil back onto the seed as he reached the end of the stand, then turned and started along the wide line George had just laid. "And speaking of William and James, have you all received any word from them recently?"

"Not in a couple of weeks. Last we heard, they had joined up with the main body and were forming into their different divisions, drilling all the time. It was rumored that they were going to be moving north, but Will said he wasn't sure."

"He is probably quite aggravated with that, the waiting and not knowing what will happen."

"He didn't say, but I reckon so. He was itching to join up, and all that drilling they been doing I bet he finds down right annoying."

"He ain't drilling anymore," a voice called.

Peter and George turned sharply and found Charles striding wearily across the field, his shoulders drooping as if from a heavy load. His hat sat pushed back upon his head and his determined jaw and eyes with a far-off expression concurred with the impression of a great burden upon the man's spirit, though what that burden was remained unknown.

"I stopped by the post," Charles continued as he stepped up to George and Peter strode over to join them. "There was a letter from William. It was dated a few days old, but it had just got in yesterday."

"How is he doing?" Peter asked expectantly, though wary in light of Charles' manner.

Handing the letter to his son, Charles replied, "I do not know. Read the letter, George."

George took the papers and turned them over to the first page. Clearing his throat, he began—

Dear Ma and Pa,

I hardly know where to begin, so much has happened since I last wrote. We received word that a Federal force was moving into Virginia, led by General Irvin McDowell, and we were detached to meet him. We marched for some time, but we finally pitched at a little railroad junction in a small town called Manassas. It finally happened, we finally met the Yankees! They came over the hills in the morning light, all dressed rather smartly in their shiny blue uniforms, all stepping off together—looked mighty fine, I tell you. Everyone thought that it was going to be over quick. Even some of the gentle folk even from as far as Washington came to watch us. I thought we would all array ourselves, then some sort of delegation would be called for, but they didn't. They open fired upon us, and we shot back. You ain't never herd such awful ruckus in all your days. For a while, it seemed that the Yanks had about whooped us, and a lot of the boys had started to run. I admit, I felt like joining them myself as the blue coats kept a coming. But then, one of the other regiments rallied on one of the ridges, holding fast against the charge

*of the Yanks. Our officers rallied us and
we took up our position once again, but
a little farther back. Well, to make a
long story short, we put the Yankees to
flight. We held firm, pushing them
back, and they commenced to running.
Oh how they ran! They flung all they
could alongside the road, everything
from their blankets to brand new rifles
and sabers. I cannot tell you how much
bounty we collected. We pursued them
for a while...*

George looked up at his father, then glanced at Peter, then back again. Not one of the three spoke, the reality of what had just been read preventing rashly spoken words.

Peter felt his thumbs rubbing against his fingers. It had actually happened. They had known it would come, but to actually hear that shots had been fired and that blood had been shed changed so much. Up until that point, it had been a struggle over words. A struggle hotly infused with tension, yes, but now blood had been spilled for those words. The hopes of some for a quick end to the turmoil by a show of resistance was ended. There could be no easy resolution now.

George was the first to break the silence. "They've done it. They've actually done it..."

"Yes, they have," Charles replied huskily, his eyes not really seeing anything around him, as if he saw something beyond what lay before him there in that field. "I had prayed to God that it would not have come to this, but it has."

"What do you think this means?" Peter ventured. "I mean, this has complicated matters even more. Fort Sumter had not resulted in any deaths, but I imagine the losses for both sides from this engagement would have been great."

"I am not sure. The letter did not describe anything about how many had been killed or wounded, but I suspect you are right. I fear that this is only the beginning. The North and South were not going to settle their differences easily before, but now that lives have been lost in this conflict, it will only make them hold their views even more firmly. I tremble to think of what may follow this battle, for that is what it is. The first battle of this war between our states."

■■

Peter laid the poplar board he had pulled off the wagon onto the bench inside Samuel's shop. "I think this one will be wide enough."

Samuel pulled his folding ruler from his pocket and measured the width of the wood, then nodded. "You would be right in that. This is a good, clean board; it will do nicely."

"Thank you, sir. I thought it would." Peter stepped back to the wagon and laid hold of the top most board. Pulling it toward him, he gripped the middle of the wood and carried the board to the rack on the far side of the shop.

Samuel unfolded his ruler and made the measurement he needed upon the first board Peter had retrieved. "Yes sir, I think this set will look first rate in poplar."

"I agree. The grain in this load from the mill is especially fine."

"That it is."

As Peter returned to the wagon to select the next board, Samuel remarked, "I have been meaning to ask you, but what do you think about this conflict, this battle at Manassas Junction?"

Peter stopped in his pull of the board. Wagging his head, he resumed his action and stepped towards the stack of lumber he was placing on the rack. "I feel so many different things about it, I find it hard to put into words."

"Just try. I would like to hear."

"My first reaction was sorrow. It grieved me to hear that our differences had carried men so far that they would actually be willing to kill one another over these matters. But as I thought about what happened, I grew angry."

"Angry?"

"Yes sir, angry. Angry that these issues had driven men to this point. Angry that this will only fuel the passions of so many. I am ashamed to admit it, though, but even more than all of those things, I am angered that this has come to Virginia, to our home. There are so many of us who did not ask for this war, who wanted no part of it. People like yourself and the Taylors."

"And people like you."

"Yes sir, I would include myself in that. I think about what this war might mean for Virginia. If these battles continue to happen, it will mean that homesteads will be destroyed both by the actual fighting and by the pillaging that happens with war, as you have described to me. Furthermore, the naval blockade of all our ports will cripple our economy as time progresses. So, I am angry that a few men who desired to set up their own nation have brought this upon those of us who were simply content to continue as loyal, submissive citizens of the government."

Samuel nodded, taking up his handsaw and beginning the first downward stroke of the tool into the wood's grain. After a few successive strokes, he paused and raised his head to the young man. "From what I gather, it sounds as if you are angered by the loss of life that has already occurred, but also by the blood that may be shed in the future as well as the struggles that peace-seeking citizens of Virginia might face."

"Yes sir, that is it. Now that blood has been shed, it will feed the desire for more and more. I do not see a way for this to end well."

"It cannot," Samuel smiled softly, sorrowfully.

"Forgive me," Peter continued, "I did not mean that. I meant end before more damage can be done. I know that if it were to end today, it would not be well because of what has already occurred. But do you not think that this will go on and on and what that might mean for simple families who wanted no part of rebellion?"

"I do. I believe battles will become the majority of what we read in our papers from now on for some time. I know that things will become increasingly difficult for families. They will be seeking necessities, not comforts like we make."

"Is my anger wrong? When I see that more lives will be lost and the difficulties that are coming, should I not be angry for a just cause?"

"Your anger is not wrong as long as it does not remain as anger."

Peter dropped the board he held onto the rack and turned to face his employer. "Sir?"

"If you are angry about these things because of a righteous anger, then good. These things grieve the

Lord, and they should us as well. When our Lord Jesus saw those who disregarded God's Word and mixed their own selfish gain with the things of God, it angered Him. But the Bible tells us that godly grief, godly anger does not stay welling up inside of us. Grief leads us to repentance. Righteous anger should do the same. Do you remember what our Lord did when He was angry with the Pharisees?"

"He drove the money changers out of the Temple," Peter replied with deep emotion and conviction.

"Yes, He did, but I was thinking more of the account of the man with the withered hand. You read the Gospel of Mark, third chapter. Jesus was grieved and angered by the hardness of the Pharisees' hearts, but He healed the man with the disfigurement.

"Son, if you let the grief and anger within you settle and remain, it will turn into bitterness and hate. They will begin slowly, but they will eventually consume you." He drilled Peter's eyes. "Don't let it do that."

Peter considered the man's words, chewing his lower lip and furrowing his brow. As if unsure of his evaluation, he remarked, "So, you are telling me I need to do something. But what? If I stay, I see the struggles that await these families, here and in the rest of the South. But then, how could I go and join this fight that I have wanted nothing to do with?"

"I am not telling you that you should do either one or the other, but you will have the choice to make of whether your anger will consume and control you, or whether you are going to master it. Cain struggled with hatred and bitterness towards his brother, but the Lord said, 'sin lieth at the door. And unto thee shall be his desire, and thou shalt rule over him.' Peter, the sin of bitterness and hatred is crouching at your door. That sin mastered Cain; it must not do the same to you."

"But I do not want this war. I do not believe it is right for Virginia to have separated from the North. Yet now that we have been invaded by an army that is seeking to kill, I cannot bare to think that I am remaining behind and doing nothing while my friends are laying down their lives for the defense of our homes."

"So you are considering enlisting?"

"I don't know," the weary sigh escaped Peter's throat. "I want to stay here. I need to stay here to help with—" He caught himself, scrambling for something he could say that would not reveal his secret. "Need to stay and help those who need it on their farms."

"Yet you feel compelled to join the army."

Peter solemnly nodded. "Yes sir, I do."

Returning his own thoughtful nod, Samuel inquired, "But do you feel that it is the Lord leading you in that direction, or are you listening to that anger inside of you and to what other people are telling you?"

"I am not sure," Peter whispered. "I want to say that I am listening to the Lord, but I fear that I may be becoming swept up in passion and love for my state."

"I am glad you are trying to be honest with yourself. You can fool others, but you cannot fool yourself, nor the Lord. Until you are persuaded you need to change, I would council you to continue working on the surrounding farms, helping those who have lost their boys and fathers in this cause. But ask the Lord to help you with your anger, son. He will do it, but you must be willing to turn from it. One of my favorite passages of scripture is Psalm 37. There are numerous exhortations in it to follow the Lord and not become swept away by what we see. In it, the psalmist tells us to 'Trust in the Lord, and do good,' but he also says, 'Cease from anger, and forsake wrath.' That is what we must do. If you are angry because of what has happened, good; we should be angered by this. But we must not allow that anger to become who we are. Realize that we have a responsibility to do good and obey the Lord. Do not be afraid of where He may lead you. Turn from that anger and follow Him no matter where He leads."

CHAPTER FIFTEEN

Peter reined in his horse in front of the post office, the building casting a shadow from the October morning sun. Swinging himself from the saddle, Peter leapt to the ground, wrapped the leather straps around the hitching post, and stepped onto the wooden deck in front of the building.

"Hello, Peter!"

Turning towards the sunny voice, Peter recognized the speaker as Henry, striding towards him alongside his sisters. He tipped his hat towards them then turned his own steps in the direction of their approaching figures. "Hello, Henry. Jenny, Emily, it is a pleasure to see you all."

"It is good to see you as well," Jenny smiled. "We were just coming into town for a few things and Henry saw you pass by as we were walking."

"I needed a few things myself. It has been quite some time since I've come in, so I had a few things to purchase at the general store, and I was just about to check my mail. I don't correspond regularly with many people, but sometimes Olivia or Mother might write me."

"We were going to the post office too," Henry concurred. "We wanted to see if there was a letter from William or James."

"Well, how about that?" He looked up at Jenny. "Your father shared with me about their last letter after meeting on Sunday. It sounded like William was in good spirits still, even after these months."

"He is, and James is as well, judging from his own letter. He does not write as frequently as William does, but that may be because he is moving more with being in the cavalry."

"Maybe so."

The foursome turned and continued to the post office. As they stepped through the door, a small bell rang over their heads, announcing their entrance. The building was mostly empty, aside from the post mistress, Mrs. Walburg, and another lady from one of the surrounding farms, Rebecca Joiner.

Mrs. Walburg looked up at the sound of the bell, smiling at the newcomers. "Well, howda do, Jenny?"

"Quite well, Mrs. Walburg. And how do you find yourself?"

"Oh, sore as ever," she rubbed her shoulder. "These aching bones still giving me the devil at nights."

"Oh, I'm sorry to hear that," Jenny sympathized. "Have you found anything that helps it?"

"Aw, Doc gave me some ointment, said I had to rub it in twice a day, and it does help...if I remember it. I just find myself so busy that I forget about it when my shoulder ain't bothering me too much some mornings, but I'll pay for it at night. But," she smiled, "I don't believe that is what you came in here for."

"Well, we were going to ask if we had received any letters, but I do hope you get to feeling better. Ma sometimes makes this poultice, and she says it helps a lot—"

Mrs. Walburg waved her off as she turned to the slotted cabinet behind her. "Aw, don't you mind me. I'm just a cranky old woman. Some people accuse me of carrying on more than the truth actually may be. I know you've got a hankering to hear from your brothers. One came in since you were here last."

She faced the counter once again with a few envelopes in her hand, offering them to Jenny. "Here you go, sweetie."

Jenny accepted them gratefully, then stepped back to sort through them, examining the handwriting of each.

Peter stepped forward and cleared his throat. "Hello, Mrs. Walburg."

"Hello, Peter," she replied curtly, the friendly air fading from her voice. "What can I do for you?"

"I was wondering if I had received any letters recently, since it has been some time since I last checked."

"Mmmph," she murmured as she searched the cubbies behind her. "Let me see. I can't help but think that I might be doing more business with you if you actually were doing your duty."

"Ma'am?"

She turned back to face him. "Oh, just that if you were off with the army, you would be sending letters back to a sweetheart or something, and those letters would be a flying through here. As it is, I don't suspect many girls would want to write such letters to a boy afraid to take a stand for his country."

"Mrs. Walburg," he replied measuredly, checking the swelling frustration within him, "I have determined to follow the Lord and His leading, and as of yet, I do not feel that it is His will for my life that I should enlist in the army. And as to writing to or having a sweetheart, one does not exist for me, even before war erupted. That is something else I am leaving to the Lord's timing."

"Uh-huh. Well, there was one letter for you." She handed him an envelope, almost begrudgingly. "I guess we should be prayin' that the Lord opens your eyes to the truth."

Peter took the letter, glancing down at the hand written address and froze. He knew that handwriting, but it belonged to the last person on earth he expected to get a letter from.

Mrs. Walburg eyed him curiously, suspicion marked in her expression. "Something wrong, Peter?"

"Uh, no ma'am. I, I was just noticing the hand."

"It is mighty fine. You recognize it?"

"Perhaps. I will know for sure when I read it. Thank you very much. I hope your shoulder starts doing better for you."

"Thank you."

As the bell clanged above the door, Peter left the building and strode towards his horse. Jenny and her younger siblings followed, preparing to pursue the rest of their errands.

"Is everything alright, Peter?" Jenny inquired.

"I am not sure," Peter returned, his voice low, not meeting her gaze.

"Was it what Mrs. Walburg said? She is just a lonely widow, her husband having passed a few years ago and her sons off fighting in the Confederacy—"

"No, it's not that." He finally lifted his eyes and found hers. "The letter was from my father."

"Your father?" she repeated incredulously. "You have never mentioned getting a letter from him before."

"That is because I have not. It has been over two years since I left, and my only contact with him has been through Olivia or my mother, but never to him directly. That is what took me off guard in there."

"Do you know what it could be about? I mean, did Olivia hint about anything in her last letter?"

Laying his hand upon his saddle horn, Peter mounted his horse and shook his head. "She didn't say anything that gives me any inkling about what this could be, but I'm about to find out." He tipped his hat. "You all have a fine afternoon."

Exchanging a parting wave with the Taylor trio, Peter turned his horse and kicked her into a trot. As he rode to his cabin, his mind swirled with possibilities of what the letter might contain. At first, thoughts of his father trying to renew their relationship arose before him, but he quickly dismissed the notion. He eliminated the possibility of a casual letter, since he had never received any before from him. The only possibility left was the one he feared—a letter bearing ill news of his mother or sister. He tried to assure himself that he did not know that yet, but he could not rid himself of the doubt creeping into his mind.

After putting Pat back in her stall, Peter collected his few items he had obtained in town along with the letter and strode expectantly, though anxious instead of eager, towards his cabin. Placing the dry goods upon his table, Peter sank into one of the chairs and stared at the letter in his hands. After a moment, a determined look leapt into his eye and he ripped open the seal, pulled the letter out, and read—

Nysler, Virginia

October 21st, 1861

My son, I hope this letter finds you well. A matter of urgent business has arisen that demands your attendance here at home. I pray you will come as soon as possible.

Your father,

John Brenton

Peter laid the letter upon his lap and leaned back in his chair. His father had never been one to use more words than necessary, but the ambiguous nature of the letter filled Peter with dread, confirming his earlier fears from his return home. What other possibility could there be? His eye came to rest upon the paper once again. His family's home lay a few hours to the east, though he knew he could make better time on horseback than his sister did in her carriage. He would talk with Samuel about it first thing in the morning.

■■

As he turned Pat into the flowering dogwood-lined lane that progressed to his family's plantation, Peter felt his heart beginning to beat quicker. Samuel had said that there was not much pressing work that day and he could excuse Peter, and so he had taken the ride out to answer his father's summons.

He pulled his horse to a halt and surveyed the path ahead of him, a rise in the ground before him preventing his view of the plantation. He had not been home in nearly two years. But that was not what held him back. He dreaded to think of what he might discover when he arrived at the house. Breathing a quick prayer, he bent down and patted the mare's neck. "Let's go, girl. It will not do me any good to wait."

As he crested the hill, amazement filled him as he surveyed the plantation spreading out before him, the fields of cotton and tobacco presenting a vast background to the large plantation house. Had this once been his home?

The porch of the house ran the entire length of the building, the wide steps carved out of limestone. Glistening windows figured prominently along both floors of the house, and a thin curl of smoke rose from one of the two chimneys, one on either side of the house. The lane rolled down the low slope and transitioned into a circular drive, a massive oak sheltering a solitary bench standing at the center of the curve.

As Peter pulled his horse to a halt in front of the six stone steps, a young Negro lad ran to meet him. "Massa Peter? Dat you?"

"Hello, Carter. How are you?"

"Dat is you, sure 'nough," the boy grinned. "Might I take yer horse, sir?"

Swinging himself from the saddle, Peter handed the boy the reigns. "Please, Carter. I would be obliged to you."

"Thank you, sir."

"Is my family at home? I had not written to announce my plans, but I was told to come as soon as I could."

"Yes sir, dey all here. Missus Brenton and Missus Olivia des in the house, but Massa Brenton is out checkin' on da fields. Shall I tell him dat you are here, sir?"

"That will be fine. Thank you."

"Thank you, sir."

As Carter led the horse to the barn, Peter climbed the steps and, with a sinking heart, rapped upon the mahogany door. A slave girl, slightly younger than himself answered his knock. As she took in the young man, recognition flooded her face. "Massa Peter? What you be doing here?" Then catching herself, "Oh, excuse me sir. Of course, it ain't none of my business. Missus Brenton always a'saying dat I talk too freely. You are welcome here, of course."

"It is no trouble, Eliza. My father sent for me and so I came to answer his call. I just gave my horse to

Carter, and your brother said he would inform my father that I had arrived. Is my mother up yet?"

"Yes sir, she is. She and Missus Olivia are in da sitting room."

"Fine." Peter followed Eliza across the carpeted floor, his own dirt floor coming to mind. As if he still had trouble remembering everything, Peter surveyed the vast portraits of his ancestors on the wall, the fine drapery from the windows, the well-polished vases upon side tables. His sister's words from her visit last November came to his mind—*Can you really expect me to spend a night in a place like your cabin?* No, Olivia definitely could not. And until he had determined to leave, he had never considered that he would either.

Eliza stepped into the doorway and cleared her throat. "Ahem, Missus Brenton?"

"Yes, what is it?" Peter heard his mother return.

"Excuse me ma'am, Missus Olivia, but you ladies have yourselves a visitor."

"A visitor? Who on earth could that be? Here, let me have her card."

"Uh, begging your pardon ma'am, it ain't a her, it's a him. It is your son." She stepped aside and the young man filled the doorway.

His mother sat upon a lush, cushioned couch, her elegant gown settled about her as she read a book she had recently started. Olivia sat across from her, engaged in a small piece of embroidery. Both ladies started at his appearance, his mother dropping her book and raising her hand to her mouth, drawing in sharply. Olivia's eyes widened significantly, then a teasing smirk formed upon her face. "Well, I never expected to see you here."

"It is good to see you as well, Olivia," he bowed slightly, then turned to face the older lady sitting upon the other couch. "Hello, Mother."

"Peter," she whispered, rising slowly from her seat. "What are you doing here?"

"Father sent for me, telling me there was a matter of urgent business I needed to attend to. Are you well?"

"Yes, I am fine. I am just excited, that is all." She stepped towards her son, and with tears forming in her pale, blue eyes, drew him into an embrace. "I did not know that you were coming, and your entrance took me by surprise."

She released him and held him at arm's length. "And how are you?" she smiled, sniffing. "Are you well?"

"I am well, thank you."

"You say that, but—my! Look at you. You've gotten scrawny and, is this what you wear now?"

"Oh no, mother," Olivia giggled teasingly. "Those are much nicer than the drab country clothes he was wearing when I have visited him. And you should see his cabin. Why, it is simply dreadful!"

"Are you taking care of yourself?" his mother inquired, concern filling her voice. "You look like you have not been eating enough and—"

"No, I am fine. I tell you the truth, I truly am. My cabin is sufficient for my needs, and it is not too drafty in the winter. I eat enough, and I take supper with some of my neighbors when I can, and they feed me very well. I stay active enough, and have been getting along fine."

"Ah, well. I am pleased to hear you find yourself well, but are you as well as you could be? I have not been out to your place, but from what Olivia has described to me, it sounds positively frightful. Are you sure you are eating enough food?"

"Yes, Mother," he smiled at her concern. "I am sure."

"Alright then. I suppose you know what is best for you." She sighed. "I knew your father said he had an important matter to discuss with you, but I did not know you were coming, not this soon. Does he know that you are here?"

"I believe so. When I gave my horse to one of the boys out front, he said he would inform him."

"Your horse? You rode all this way on horseback? Olivia tells me it takes hours to get to Chesson!"

"Yes ma'am. It was not too hard of a journey, and I enjoyed the ride."

Olivia rolled her eyes. "I tried to tell you, Mother, Peter's a good old country fellow now. No more of these carriages, no more slaves preparing him plenteous meals—"

"And no more letters telling me when you were coming," a voice boomed from the doorway behind them.

Cringing, Peter turned to meet the voice. "Hello, Father."

John Brenton towered in the doorway, his broad shoulders filling his tailored suit admirably. His eyes remained rigidly fixed upon his son, though his lips formed the faintest hint of a smile. "Hello. I thought you might respond to let me know when you were coming."

"Your letter said to come as soon as possible, and so I assumed that it would be better if I came immediately rather than sending a note ahead of me and waiting several days," he attempted to explain.

"Well, a reply would have been the proper thing to do, but you are here anyway. Jethro," he turned into the hallway, "bring the carriage around to the door."

"The carriage?" his wife repeated. "John, why do you need the carriage? Your son has just arrived—"

"I know he just arrived, Harriet. He is going to accompany me to see something I have to show him. Are you ready, Peter?"

"Yes sir."

The drive passed with an odd mix of silence and disjointed bits of conversation. John would abruptly ask a question about Peter's situation and community, and once his son would answer, would lapse back into silence with a nod of affirmation. Peter considered his father's behavior peculiar, though not entirely without explanation. When he had left, their parting had been tense, and without hardly any communication since that time, he did not expect their meeting to be comparable to his conversations with his sister.

Drawing to the end of a small lane, the driver pulled the carriage to a halt in front of a small, though elegant, house. John opened the door and motioned for Peter to follow his example.

Peter complied, his curiosity sparked by their destination. "I do not remember this home. Are we paying a call upon someone I know?"

"No, this house is empty."

"Empty?" His father was becoming even more and more curious.

"Yes, empty. You see, Peter, I did not want you to leave my home. I love you, you are my son. I could not abide your wild ideas about slavery, but I had not wished for them to come between us. Even after you left, I regretted many of the things I said to you when we parted and I told you to leave my house if you were going to stubbornly hold such views, but I have continued to love you. However, I have not brought you here to reopen our old argument.

"You see, I know you are a very conscientious man, and I imagine with much of the misunderstanding of the war, you have been struggling with whether you can support such a fight. I do not wish or desire you to enlist in the army. It is too dangerous, neither is it your place. As I said, you have your convictions, and I infer that you find it difficult to embrace the views of the Confederacy by enlisting in the army, am I right?"

"Yes sir," Peter began slowly, "you are. In part, anyway."

John nodded. "As I thought. I have asked you here because I think I have a solution and I have a proposal. Now, what I am about to tell you must not be repeated to anyone, you understand? This has come from my connections in the government, but it must not be spread around.

"The Confederate government is beginning to realize that this war may take longer than we originally anticipated. We also realize that if all of us plantation owners leave our homes to fight, it will leave the Negros with no one to manage them. True, the foremen might remain, but the man of authority will be gone. And so, a draft is being formed."

The Choice

"A draft? You mean, to force men to serve in the army?"

"Yes, but hear me out. They are forming a draft. I do not know when this conscription act will go into effect, but it could be very soon. But here is where the part that concerns us comes in. There is also a bill that will be presented to Congress soon that will exempt any man who owns over twenty slaves from any military service.

"And this is my proposition to you. I understand that you wish all slaves to be free, and that is your conviction. I know you struggle with whether you can in good conscience enlist in the military, and I do not want you to. Therefore, I am willing to make you an offer. I will give you this house and twenty-two slaves, some of my own and some I will purchase, for you to have until this war is over. When this conflict has dissolved, you will simply sign them back over to me and you will be free. You are not propagating the institution of slavery, since the slaves do not really belong to you; think of them merely as on loan. However, this will provide you with a legitimate excuse for avoiding any service in the Confederate military. I am not asking you to make a decision right now, I know you prefer to think things through thoroughly before you make a choice this large. I am asking you to think about it. The offer stands, and I implore you to accept it."

CHAPTER SIXTEEN

As Peter stepped towards the open door of the small school house, the lilting tones of Jenny's voice met his ears. Apparently, some boys had been using the rear door with too great of a force, and with the boards already being in poor condition, it had begun to pull away from the casing, the joints of the panels loosening. Samuel had been requested several days earlier to find an appropriate time to repair it, but as he had several pressing jobs to finish, he had sent his young employee to complete the task. Peter did not mind, for after the students left directly, it would afford him opportunity to work alone and to sort out his troubled thoughts. His father's offer was one he knew he could not accept, but how to explain that to him was another matter. He would have nothing to do with slavery in any form, but the visit had awakened the embers of a relationship he had not known still existed.

Shifting his tool box in his hand, Peter strode up the few steps and slipped inside the building. He would have time to deal with that later. Moving softly so as not to disrupt the class, he placed his hat and coat alongside the students upon the rack at the front of the structure, then waited, listening for Jenny to pause in her lesson before stepping into the main part of the classroom.

"...continue to review those sums on page forty-three, and remember that we will have a test this Friday. Now, pull out your history books."

Peter stepped around the partition that separated the classroom from the foyer, rapping his knuckles upon the wall to announce his entrance. "Afternoon," he greeted.

Jenny turned from the blackboard and returned, "Hello. How are you?"

"Well, thank you. Mr. Kouffers sent me over to repair that door," he gestured towards the rear of the room, "and if I will not be disturbing you, I was going to start on it. I will be as quiet as I can, but I can wait if that is needed."

"Oh no, you will be fine. We do not lack much from finishing, so please, do whatever it is you need to."

"Thank you." He slipped past the last row of desks, then along the side wall as he made his way to the door that required his attention. Several of the students eyed him curiously, but a few remained doggedly fixed upon their teacher.

Flipping her own book to the appropriate page, Jenny resumed her lesson. "Turn to page seventy-three..."

As he surveyed the damaged door, Peter laid his tools upon the wooden floor as noiselessly as he could. Straightening, he stroked his chin. The door was in worse repair than Samuel had intimated, or perhaps knew, since he himself had not come to inspect it. The bottom panels would need to be completely replaced, and with the separation of the uppermost ones, he deemed an entirely new door should be made. However, since they had only been summoned to repair it, he would do the best he could, submitting his opinion to Samuel at the shop the following day.

The handle had become loose, and since it was practically a soundless task, he opted to start with it. He knew the school would let out in thirty minutes or so, but he wished to distract as little as possible from the class. Pulling a screwdriver from the wooden box, he set about his task.

While he worked, he listened as Jenny taught on the still recent Mexican War, only a few decades past, writing key dates and names upon the blackboard as she spoke. He could tell her passion for instructing children from her voice, and though he had known she enjoyed her own work, her enthusiasm impressed him. Chesson had chosen their teacher wisely, he reflected.

"...and now," Jenny emphasized, the intonation of her voice calling attention to her words, "let us review our list of presidents and their terms of office."

Though he faced away from the class, Peter grimaced. He had not thought before that point to ask how she handled history, whether she taught both of the Union and the Confederacy, or if she only focused upon their southern nation. As Jenny continued, he realized she was following the path he feared she would.

She began writing and calling the names of presidents, beginning with Washington, Adams,

Jefferson, and on up through their own time. Occasionally she would pause after mentioning a name, asking for a particular student to answer the question of their length and terms of office, or ask the children to answer which President came next in the list.

In answer to his teacher's question, Robert replied, "Buchanan was the fifteenth, 1857 through 1861."

"Very good," Jenny encouraged, writing the name upon the board behind her. "And now we come to the—"

"Our honorable Jefferson Davis," one of the older boys interrupted, deep reverence in his voice.

Peter cocked his head slightly towards the class as Jenny returned gently, "No, Caleb, I'm afraid that is not right. President Davis is the first president of our Confederacy, but he is not the sixteenth one of the United States of America. Does someone else know the answer?"

A young girl on the front row meekly raised her hand. "President Abraham Lincoln."

Caleb spat loudly upon the floor in disgust, attracting the attention of his teacher like a magnet. "Caleb, please—that is inappropriate."

"No it ain't, ma'am. My Pa does it all the time."

"Your father may have his own views—"

"Mine does it too," a boy about Henry's age piped up across the room. "He says that Lincoln ain't fit to hold office 'tall."

"You got that right," Caleb returned. "Someone ought to give that baboon a good swift kick in the rear!"

"Boys," Jenny's stern voice interrupted. "We are talking about the Presidents. We owe these men respect, regardless of our own personal opinions."

"But why?" Caleb shot back, scorn etching itself upon his face. "Pa said he's just the leader of those dern Yankees. 'Course, Pa didn't say dern; he—"

"Caleb!" Peter barked, jumping to his feet and striding to the boy's desk.

Stepping directly in front of him, Peter continued loud enough for the entire class to hear. "Your teacher has just explained to you that you are to respect these men. Though President Lincoln is not the leader of our country, he does hold the highest office in his own. Furthermore, do not use those words I know your father attributes to our Northern neighbors, and definitely not here in class. Do you understand me?"

"It don't matter. Everybody knows they ain't nothing but a pack of thievin' coyotes who don't deserve no better, and Pa says—"

"Your father possesses views that he would do well to keep to himself. All men are created equal, do you all not remember that?" he turned towards the rest of the class. "I know Miss Taylor has taught you the

Declaration of Independence, and though it is not entirely our nation's document any longer, it was the words upon which our fathers started their new lives upon this continent. The Lord has seen fit to make men in a variety of forms, sizes, and even color, but no man is of less value than another. We are all the same in the eyes of the Lord. No matter who tells you otherwise, always remember that."

"You sound so high and mighty," Caleb folded his arms, "but you ain't."

"I am only speaking the truth," Peter turned to face him.

"Yeah, well," the boy leaned forward in his seat. "You know what my Pa says about you? He says you're a yellow-bellied coward who is the disgrace of this valley!"

Stunned, Peter stared down at the boy as the silence fell even heavier upon the room. He had no idea that Caleb's father, Randal Smith, thought so poorly of him. Over the past several months, he had felt his community's opinion of his character slowly turning against him, but he had not realized that some members had taken it so far.

Choosing his words carefully, Peter replied slowly, "Your father and I have our differences of opinion on several matters, but that does not negate the truth of what I said."

"And remember," Jenny added with cheeks flushed with embarrassment and indignation, "this nation was formed because our leaders believed in the right of each state to govern itself, each having that equal right. As long as the North was willing to respect that, the southern states had no quarrel with them."

Peter returned to where he had laid his tools as she continued, "As I mentioned earlier, remember we have that arithmetic test on Friday, so make sure you take your time and go over your lessons thoroughly. Class dismissed."

Occupying himself with repairing what he could of the door amidst the general scramble and commotion of the students collecting their books and bursting out of the room, Peter could not shake Caleb's words from his mind. He had been praying diligently and earnestly about whether he should take up arms for the Confederacy, but he worried of what message his enlisting might send to His friends, his father, and to the community. Now with the knowledge of what men like Randal Smith, and probably Carson Jones, were saying about him, he feared that they would interpret his action as his succumbing to their pressure and not from a genuine conviction to follow only the Lord, and the thought filled him with frustration.

No matter which choice he made, he would be misunderstood, scorned, and maligned. If he stayed in Chesson, he would be seen as a cowardly Union sympathizer. If he joined the Confederate army, he would be viewed as a boy who could not even make up his own mind. If he enlisted for the Northern cause, he would be called a traitor. The third option was one he had almost entirely rid himself of considering, but the first two seemed to pull him with equal, yet opposing force. And either way, there was the problem of explaining his choice to his father....

Closing her books upon her own desk, Jenny stepped across the room to where Peter squatted, bent over his work. "I am so sorry for what Caleb Smith said. I had no idea—"

"There is no need to apologize," Peter smiled softly, rising from his task. "It was nothing you did, or even something you could control. Mr. Smith, Mr. Jones, and those like them have their own views, and that is between me and them. I had heard Caleb's father speak against the Union before, and I was afraid of what he was fixing to say, and that is why I stepped in. Please, do not feel that you have to apologize for anything."

"I had no idea they thought that of you...I just cannot believe it." She wagged her head as her eyes filled with compassion. "They know that you are trying to follow the Lord, so why will they not let you alone?"

"They are blinded by their own passion. Please, do not trouble yourself about me. Mr. Kouffers, your family, and others still treat me with kindness, and most important, the Lord has been by my side. I know He will continue to do so." He glanced towards the front of the schoolroom where Emily stood beside Henry and Robert, each slipping into their coats.

Nodding towards her siblings, Peter commented, "Do not wait for me to finish up here; I will close up when I am done."

"Are you sure? I could work on grading homework or preparing a lesson."

"I am sure. I think your siblings are ready to head home. I will be fine."

"Well then, good evening."

"Good evening."

As Jenny joined her siblings on their way out of the school, Peter turned back to his task, shaking his own head. He was deeply grateful for the compassion and kindness of his neighbors, even if the rest of the valley was turning against him. He did not lack much from completing what he could on the door, and he busied himself with securing the casing once again, driving new nails to secure it in place,.

With the door temporarily repaired and locked securely, Peter collected his tools and left the one-room structure, latching the main door behind him as he exited. He slipped the leather strap of the tool box around his shoulder and turned his steps towards the rest of the buildings in the small town. He needed to purchase more nails and a little flour, and it was light enough yet to permit him to make the detour before returning home.

Only a few other customers were in the general store, and Peter quickly found the items he needed.

Laying them upon the counter, he greeted the clerk. "How are you, Mr. Mason?"

"Tolerable enough," he replied in his deep base voice. Seth's uncle was a man of few words.

He added the prices up, tallying the total upon a scrap of paper. Lifting his eyes towards his customer, he informed, "That will be five eighty-three."

Peter's brow furrowed together as he considered the amount. "Mr. Mason," he began slowly, "I do not mean to sound presumptuous, but last time I had purchased these items from you, the price was a good deal lower."

The clerk nodded. "It was, you are right."

Peter feared he knew the meaning behind the man's words, though he hoped he was incorrect. "Is there…has something happened to raise the prices?"

"Unfortunately, there is. There is a war going on, and the government needs all the metal they can lay their hands upon. They have rifles, canteens, and cannons to manufacture, and that leaves only that much less material to make those things needed by the common citizen. As a matter of business, with supply and demand, the prices have risen as a result."

Indignation rose within Peter's chest, though he tried to restrain himself from allowing it to appear in his expression. It was the very thing Samuel and he had talked about for months—that the war would take its toll on the average citizens who wanted nothing to do with the war. Granted, the price was not a large increase, nothing that would cause him to suffer, but he feared what the prolonged conflict would do in the future as materials became even more scarce.

He pulled a few bills from his pocket and handed them to the clerk. Soon after Virginia had formed the Confederacy, he had been required to turn all of his American bills in for the new national currency. It had not mattered then, but as more and more business men refused to accept anything but Confederate money, an individual found that his paper which would have made him rich in the North was worthless in the South. It was Confederate money or nothing.

Mr. Mason counted the few coins change back into Peter's hand and wished him a good day. Peter thanked him, then turned out of the shop. Laying his recent purchases in his box slung around his shoulder, he started the several mile journey to his cabin, a weight settling upon his heart even more.

As he walked, he knew the crisis of his decision was drawing near. If he stayed, he would need a way to prove he desired to be a loyal citizen, regardless of which ever government was in power. Yet he knew that the scenes he had witnessed that day were only the precursors of what awaited him if he remained in Chesson. If he chose to join the army, he desired a way to leave honorably. He did not want to think about what might be said about him if he left to enlist, not with what was being circulated about him just then. Furthermore, if he did join the Confederate army, what would Samuel do without him? Even more important, what about the Taylors' and the Underground?

He paused upon the lane he walked along, his thumbs fumbling with their respective fingers. Spreading his hands out before him, palms upwards, he lifted his eyes towards the cloudless sky and pleaded, "What do You want me to do?"

CHAPTER SEVENTEEN

"...so I reckon once we get that field chopped, we might split a few rails," Charles Taylor explained as he walked towards his family's barn with Peter, George, and Robert.

"Them cows been a busting fences like crazy," expounded George, wagging his head. "We've about used up the last of the rails we had from last fall."

"I suspect we'll be able to cut a few more. This field should not take us too long," his father returned. He glanced over at Peter who walked along in a preoccupied manner. He had been unusually silent since he had arrived that morning, and his manner as of late threatened to lapse back into his former withdrawal. "Are you feeling alright, Peter?"

"Yes sir. I am fine."

"Something on your mind?"

"There are a few things I have been contemplating, but I will be fine." He tried to smile reassuringly. "I often have things I ponder while I work."

"Is it something you want to discuss? I know I often am able to think clearer when I just talk with someone about issues I am facing."

"I appreciate that, sir, but..." his eye drifted towards Robert walking by his father's side.

Charles followed Peter's gaze, comprehending the unspoken objection. Patting his son's shoulder gently, he suggested, "Robert, you and George go on ahead and get everything ready. Peter and I will join you in a moment."

"Yes sir." The two boys continued on their path while Charles slowed his pace, Peter matching his stride.

When the boys had passed out of earshot, Charles turned towards his young neighbor. "Now, what is on your mind?"

Peter searched the ground, as if he would find the words he sought among the grass at his feet. Finally, looking up, he began, "Mr. Taylor, I have been meaning to ask you about this for some time now, something I have been struggling with ever since we received word from William about Manassas. This may sound foolhardy, but I ask you to hear me out."

"Go ahead, son. Take your time."

"Quite frankly," Peter sighed, "I am finding it exceedingly difficult to reconcile feelings toward Virginia with our work in the Underground. I am still persuaded that slavery is wrong, and I earnestly wish to free as many slaves as we can. I feel that it is what we must do as Christians.

"But now that the North has invaded our state and our country men are firing upon one another, I feel compelled to put an end to this killing and destruction of our homes, our homes in Virginia and in the rest of our nation. I think war is terrible, and I had prayed it would not come to this, but the fact of the matter is that war has come. I know that one man joining the fight will not determine the tide of the war, but then again, I also know that one man's work is not going to free all the slaves in this country.

"What I keep coming back to is that men like ourselves now have two issues we are facing. On the one hand, we are contesting against the institution of slavery and those who wish to perpetuate it. On the other, we are threatened by the Federal army and the destruction of this land. We are pressed from two directions, from all sides actually. I do not know which is the bigger threat, or which should require more attention and protection against. I know that there are those who will not take up arms against the North, for whatever reason, be it age or the necessity of caring for a family. But I am not constrained by either of those. I am young and able, I have no family to provide for, and I feel ashamed that I am staying behind here and waiting while men like your sons are off in defense of this land."

Charles nodded slowly, stroking his greying beard. "So, if I understand you correctly, I infer that you are considering enlisting in the army."

"I am afraid so, sir. I feel compelled to join others like William and James to defend this land against those who would destroy it. It does not come from hatred, but I do feel a responsibility to protect Virginia and the rest of our nation, and do my part to end this war.

"Yet I feel a duty to remain here and work on the Underground. I have given myself to helping free the slaves, giving them safe passage from your home to the next depot, and if I enlisted, I would be removing that protection from them. I do not know which to choose. I feel a duty in both directions, but I cannot tell where I must turn and put my focus and my energy."

Charles refrained from commenting as they continue to walk, his head bent, his brow furrowed. After a moment, he softly asked, "The protection that you believe you would be removing, tell me, where did it come from?"

"Sir?"

Charles raised his head to meet his neighbor's gaze. "Your work in the Underground, giving safe passage. Were you the one protecting the slaves, or was it God? Ultimately, that is. I know the Lord was using you as His vessel in that work, but did you not trust in Him for protection and not in your own ability?"

"Yes sir," Peter returned slowly. "I did pray for the Lord to shield us and help me deliver the runaways safely to the next safe house."

"Exactly," Charles nodded. "You see, we have hid slaves here for years before you came to help us, and if the Lord should lead you somewhere else, He will continue to provide. Do not elevate yourself, not saying you are, but do not think so highly of yourself that you believe that the Underground will not be able to continue without your aid. We believe this work is from the Lord, and He has blessed it so far, and I am persuaded He will continue to give success to our efforts. I know you read the Word and that you seek the Lord earnestly in prayer. Continue to do so. If He should convict you that you should enlist, so be it. The Lord will meet our needs. We have not always had a conductor before, and we may not need one now. But even if we do, the Lord will provide. I may start making the runs if it seems necessary, but I trust the Lord to show us. You be obedient to how He leads you, and trust Him to direct our paths."

"You would make the runs? What about your family? Your farm? You are already so busy with things here, and if you were to—"

Charles raised a hand to stay the objection. "Peter, we still serve the God who gave manna to the Israelites, parted the waters, and fed Elijah by ravens. The Lord will provide for us. He may equip me with the strength I need to do the work, or He might multiply my time as I labor here on the farm, so that I would be able to lead the runaways. Or, He may raise someone else up to help us. He may even protect the slaves without any human help. He doesn't need us," Charles chuckled softly. "The Lord is in control. I do not mean to sound like I am avoiding reality or am blind to the needs of our situation. There are real issues and questions that we will have to face. But that should not hinder you from following the Lord's leading."

"I do not know for sure whether He is indeed leading me to enlist in the army. This objection of my work with the Underground kept me from fully considering it as an option."

"You are wise to think through how your own actions will affect others, especially those you are closely connected with, but do not let this stop you."

"Thank you, sir," Peter whispered.

After a moment of silence, having waited for Peter to continue, Charles further inquired, "Is there anything else bothering you?"

"Yes sir. Another issue I had with joining the Confederacy is how the decision may be viewed by others."

"In what way?"

"Well, I was opposed to secession, and though I was not vocal about it very much, many in Chesson know about it. There are those who do not miss an opportunity to try and remind me of my lack of dutifulness to my state, insinuating that I am a coward and a bum, content to feed off of everyone else. I am concerned that if I was to join the Confederacy—not saying that I will—what people might say. They might think that I finally just gave into their pressure. I would not be, but they might infer that I was since they would not know that I was acting only as a result of the Lord's leading me in that direction."

"I commend you for considering how your actions might be interpreted, but let me ask you, do those people who cause you concern rightly understand your motives for your current and past decisions?"

"No," Peter conceded. "I have not considered that before, but you are right. They do not."

Charles nodded. "Mmmph. That has not kept you from following the Lord up to this point, and I urge you, do not let it in the future. Do you remember Paul's rebuke to Peter with the issue at Galatia?"

"About when Peter left the Gentiles he had previously ate with when other Jews came from Jerusalem?"

"That is it. Peter knew that there was no distinction between Jews and Gentiles, and for a while, he was obedient to the Lord in that he ate with the Gentiles and their food. Yet when others came—those whom he was afraid of losing his good standing with— he tried to revert back to his old ways and acted as if it was wrong to eat with the Gentiles. Paul confronted him quite sternly on the matter, saying that he should not try to please men or force the Gentiles to live under the law.

"We do not live to please men. It is wise to consider how our action might offend others and, if they do not go against our conscience, to change our behavior around those people just for that moment. But when it comes to obedience to the Lord and His

Spirit, how men might misinterpret our actions should not stop us from following the Lord."

"So you are saying that I should join the Confederacy?"

"No, I did not say that. That is a decision between you and the Lord. All I am pointing out is that you should not let what others might or might not think keep you from obeying God. Follow Him, and Him alone. You understand?"

"Yes sir."

Charles smiled and patted the back of Peter's shoulder. "Now, let's get this field ready to go."

■■■

Peter sank to the ground, rested his back against the trunk of the oak, and bent his head upon his chest. It was the place he always climbed to in order to think, and with everything he had seen and heard over the past week or two, time devoted to serious and intense thought was certainly called for.

His father's offer from the previous week had not needed much consideration to refuse. Objections to his acceptance of the proposal were numerous and varied. First, to accept was to essentially reverse his convictions without the Lord's leading. He would be perpetuating an institution he knew was conducted in sin.

Furthermore, the proposal was based upon a bill that awaited presentation and might or might not be accepted, a bill that would excuse him from a service that it demanded other men to fulfill. Peter could not do that, even if he was neutral to the issue of slavery.

However, the offer had awakened Peter to the truth concerning his relationship with his family. He had previously known where he stood with his sister and his mother, but his father's offer to provide an escape for him from military service, even at his own expense, surprised Peter. He had thought their relationship had, for all practical purposes, ended when he had refused to bow to his father's demands. Yet this simply was not the case.

Peter had not expressed it to Charles, but his father was one of the people that concerned him most in terms of misconstruing his actions. He had already taken poorly to Peter's decision to break all ties with the institution of slavery, putting it mildly. If Peter now rejected his father's offer and engaged in the very action his father wished to protect him from, he feared what it might do to the relationship that he had recently rediscovered.

And even with the matters he had discussed with Charles Taylor, Peter had not fully reached a decision, specifically with the Underground work. If he fought to protect Virginia, was he fighting to continue slavery? But if he did not enlist, would the war destroy many of the routes of the escape network while he stayed in his own comfortable valley?

Peter sighed and opened his Bible to the passage he kept referring back to. He smoothed the pages and began reading Romans, Chapter Thirteen. As he reached verse four, his eye remained fixed upon the small words of the page, unable to move on—

> For he is the minister of God to thee for good. But if thou do that which is evil, be afraid; for he beareth not the sword in vain: for he is the minister of God, a revenger to execute wrath upon him that doeth evil.

"An avenger of evil," Peter softly mused aloud to himself, resting his head against the rough bark of the trunk behind him. Yes, there was much evil in his country. The evil of slavery pervaded the entire South, but also the evil of his countrymen killing one another over issues of state loyalty. He had not thought it best to break with the Union, but Peter condemned the North for trying to force Virginia and the other states to return. The South had not rebelled, at least, not in the sense of starting an uprising. They had made every effort to do so peacefully, only firing upon Fort Sumpter after extensive communication that had brought no change. And even then, the South Carolinians had not even killed a single American citizen in the fort.

The issue was not in finding evil that needed to be avenged. The problem lay in deciding which evil the

Lord was calling him to oppose at that time. If he stayed behind, he could not feel at peace knowing others were fighting to protect his land from those who were destroying it. Yet if he left to enlist and they were victorious over the North, what might happen to the institution of slavery?

His eye fell onto the page again. The apostle was writing of the government and its ministry of rewarding those who did good and revenging itself against the evil. That revenge, the Scripture said, involved taking up the sword. Not for personal vengeance, but as part of the government's institution of protecting and punishing.

Is that not what is called for now? He inquired of himself. There were those who demanded protection, and his government was calling for those to join them in that defense. The North had no right to force the South to remain in the Union, even though Peter wished that the Southern states would, and therefore, he felt the invasion of Virginia was an evil that fell under the government's jurisdiction in this passage from Romans.

Yet the issue of slavery still presented it objection to his mind. Was it worth risking what the future might hold? Peter gazed into the valley, his eye coming to rest upon the Taylor's cabin.

Charles had reminded him that the Lord still held the future and that no amount of worrying would change anything, but it would hinder him from being used of the Lord at that time. Slavery was an issue that would have to be dealt with regardless of Peter's decision to enlist or not. There would be difficulties if the Confederates were victorious, he had said, but he believed that they would not change significantly from their current situation. Charles had assured Peter that the Lord would provide for their needs, no matter what government would be triumphant, either the one in Washington or the one in Richmond.

The words on the page directed his attention once again. *Bear the sword,* he read. But was that for him? Was he to take up the sword for the government? He glanced towards the valley once again and felt himself pulled in a direction he had been so unwilling to embrace.

"Dear Father," he whispered, "I know that You are my Guide and my Counselor. I have prayed for You to lead me in the way that I should go, and I believe I know what You are calling me to do. Please, I ask of You to give me the wisdom to know for sure, to know without a doubt. I do not want to choose wrongly. I ask to know Your will, and I beseech You for the courage to follow that guidance, no matter the cost."

CHAPTER EIGHTEEN

The late October sun made a show of warming the Virginian air as Peter flicked the reins of his wagon as he drove through the small collection of stores and businesses in the heart of Chesson. The cold, North wind chilled the air more so than usual for that time of year, and Peter wondered whether it was a sign of the winter that was fast approaching. He had just finished delivering a new cabinet in the doctor's office beside the general store. The old one had been built with the structure, but as time and ample use had worn the piece, it had deteriorated into an object of little more use than anything beyond an eye sore to the doctor and his clients. The job had been one of the few that Peter and Samuel were occupied with, so the project had not taken long to complete.

His time on the side of the mountain the previous week had nearly settled in Peter's mind the decision he had wrestled with for so long. As he discussed his dilemma more fully with Samuel in the days that followed, continuing to devote large periods of time on his knees, the path he was to take had slowly came into focus. As he had prayed, meditated on the Scriptures, and sought the counsel of other godly men, he had become persuaded that the Lord was leading him to take up arms in defense of his land. He would not be fighting to defend slavery, but since that was not what the war was about, it was not an issue. Slavery would remain an issue to be wrestled with, but this threat from the North was one that demanded immediate attention. Whatever the differences between the North and the South, it did not call for slaughter, but that was what the Federal army was bringing, and Peter felt called to do his part to prevent that from spreading even farther South. He knew that by joining the Confederacy he would not make a noticeable difference in history, but he could not remain at home—not when the Lord was leading him otherwise.

A gathering in front of the post office caught Peter's eye as he rode, directing his curious attention. Three men sat upon their horses in the midst of a growing crowd, their coats pulled tight about them as if from a hard ride. One of the three was accompanying his words with emphatic hand gestures, though he sat too far distant for Peter to determine what was being said. As he approached, the sharp, gravelly voice gradually became more distinguishable. One of the other two happened to spot Peter approaching on his wagon and raised a glove hand towards him and called, "You there, boy! Come here."

Peter nodded, apprehension swelling within him. Pulling his horse to a stop, he lowered himself from the seat and strode to meet the man who had hailed him.

The man who had spoken to the crowd previously turned towards him as he drew near. A suspicious glint in his eye, he inquired in a voice that dripped with hatred, "We have come from North Carolina, sent by a Mr. Davidson, an owner of a prominent plantation in the Northern part of the state. Four days ago, he became aware of five of his slaves having escaped. A reward has been posted for their capture, and we have come north, following their trail. There has been little we have found to go on, and so we came here. As I was telling these fine folks before you arrived, I know that you all are loyal citizens of the Confederacy and are willing to do what may be called for. Have you seen any sign of these slaves? Three men, a young woman, and a boy?"

Peter's mind immediately flashed to the signal quilt he had seen flapping at the Taylor's home as he had traveled his way to Samuel's shop that morning, but he replied, "No sir, I can't say that I have."

"That a fact? Well, if you or your wife should happen to see them or know of where they may be, you will report them, won't you?"

Hesitantly, Peter answered, "I am not married, sir."

"You're not?" The man exchanged a look with his companions, then turned his narrowing eyes back upon Peter and leaned low in his saddle. "Do you mean to tell me that you, an able-bodied man with no family responsibilities are slouching at your own little cabin while there are others who have left home, farm, and family to give their blood for your sorry, worthless hide?"

"I have not shirked my duty, sir. I have—"

"Oh, is that so? What is your occupation? A doctor? Preacher?"

One of the older men of the crowd spoke up, disdain in his own voice. "He is only a cabinet apprentice."

Fire flickered in the slave catcher's eye as he surveyed Peter. "A cabinetmaker, eh? Very well, and I suppose you have no Union sympathies, either."

"No sir."

"So you say. Listen, regardless of how much I want to string you up right here, you have not committed a crime...yet. But if you were to know of these runaway slaves and fail to aid in their capture, you will be committing a felony. Do I make myself clear?"

"Yes sir."

"Very well then."

Trying to appear as if he had no cause for concern, Peter returned to his wagon and resumed his former journey home. It was his first encounter with a slave catcher, but he knew beyond any doubt that the man he had just spoken with would stop at nothing until he had found the slaves he sought. His search would be ruthless, just as Nathan and William had warned him it would be.

As he passed the Taylor's cabin, resting in its serene atmosphere as it had nearly every other time he had passed their home, Peter's mind raced to the danger that might soon come upon the family. He had yet to tell the Taylors of his decision to enlist, and though Charles had assured him that he must not let the Underground hold him back, Peter felt himself question his decision, his determination waning. If these slave catchers had come, what might the future hold? And, could he ask the Taylors to face that threat?

He flicked the reins on his horse. The Taylors had engaged in the Underground work long before he had come. They knew the risks, Charles had said, and they trusted the Lord to provide and protect. With a silent prayer for steadfastness, Peter determined to do the same.

Reaching his own place, Peter stabled his horse, Pat, and surveyed his barn one last time. "Goodbye, old girl." He patted the horse's side. "George or Robert will probably be by for you here in another day or so. They'll take care of you, I'm sure."

In his cabin, he smothered the remaining embers of his fire and retrieved his rifle. He stowed the last slices of cornbread and a few ears of corn in his knapsack and slung it over his shoulder. Pulling the cabin door closed behind him, Peter turned and started for the woods leading to the Taylor's farm.

The sun was beginning to set as Peter rapped upon the back door of his neighbor's cabin. Loressa answered his knock with a welcoming smile. "Why, I declare, Mr. Peter—why you a'callin back here and not round front?"

Slipping into the cabin, Peter explained, "I'm sorry, but I did not want to come down the lane. I needed to come quietly. Is Mr. Taylor at home?"

"Yes, he is," Loressa responded slowly, perplexed. "I believe he is in the dining room."

"Peter, that you?" Charles called through the doorway that divided the kitchen from the rest of the house.

"Yes sir, it is."

Charles appeared in the doorway, concern filling his face. "What is the matter?"

"Two issues, sir. I am on my way to make my next run, but I needed to warn you. When I was in town this afternoon, I encountered three slave catchers. They were looking for some runaways, and these men are ruthless. They will be cruel and merciless, and that is why I have come now. They were quite forceful in demanding information from those who had gathered, and though I did not hear anything that should cause you concern, I thought you should be made aware of their presence in Chesson."

"I appreciate that. Thank you. I am not afraid, but I will be watching for them if they should come. Was there anything else?"

"Yes sir." Peter took a deep breath. "I have decided to enlist. I have considered your counsel, and have been praying diligently about the matter. Samuel Kouffers has also discussed the matter with me, and his words were very similar to yours. I have been wrestling with this question for several months, seeking what the Lord would have me to do. But as I was praying about it over the past few days, I felt the Lord convict me that my place now is with the army. This is my last time conducting until I return."

"You are leaving tonight?" Charles' concern deepened.

"I am afraid so. I have been feeling under more and more suspicion as of late, and this afternoon, it was extremely marked. I feel that it would be best if I left immediately. I heard of a regiment that is forming about forty miles to the north, and I plan to join them as soon as I bring my charges safely to their next destination."

Charles nodded solemnly, then held out a hand towards him. "I understand. I appreciate you telling me. If the Lord is leading you this way, than I will not stand in your way. Come, at least say good-bye to the family."

Peter laid his rifle beside the door and crossed the kitchen and entered the large, open dining room of the Taylor's cabin. Emily was engaged in her usual habit of setting the table for supper, and Jenny assisted her by laying the plates at each setting. Mary sat in the offset room, finishing sewing a shirt for one of her sons, while Robert wrestled with Henry on the floor. George stood by the fireplace, poking the logs with the metal rod in his hand. They all looked up from their tasks at Peter's entrance.

"Good evening," he smiled faintly. "I hate to tell you this now, and I know that it is very abrupt, but there have been some recent factors that have affected this timing."

"Go on," Mary prodded gently, her face mimicking her husband's former concern.

"As I have been praying, I have felt the Lord convicting me that my place is with the Confederate army for the time being. I despise this war, but I despise even more what allowing it to continue may do. So, I am leaving tonight to enlist in the army."

"Tonight?" Jenny repeated, stunned.

"Yes, tonight. Right now, as a matter of fact. I wanted to stop by one last time and tell you all how dear I count you all. You have been my friends, like my own family to me over these past two years or so. No matter what may happen, I will not forget you."

Henry scrambled from the floor and ran to meet him, worry filling his nine-year-old eyes. "But you will come back, won't you, Peter?"

Peter met his gaze, trying to hide his own concern about the question. "I certainly pray so, Henry. I will be thinking about you often. Try to mind your mother and not sneak off during wash day," he attempted a tease, tousling the boy's hair.

"When do you plan to return," George inquired, laying his poker back against the stone hearth.

"I am not sure," Peter shook his head. "Maybe in a few months, if the war should end that soon. I cannot tell, only the Lord knows. I left Pat over in my stable. I want you all to have her for whatever you need. I would have brought her over tonight, but I was concerned about appearances. So George, if you would, I ask you to take care of her, bring her over here if you all have room."

"Yeah, we do, now that James is off with old June. Thank you, Peter."

"You are welcome."

Laying aside her work, Mary rose and stepped towards Peter, motherly worry etched across her face. "I had my suspicions, but this is very sudden. I'm afraid I do not know what to say."

"You have been like a second mother to me, and I thank you for that sincerely."

"You will write to us, won't you?"

"I will be sure to do so. Thank you all once again. For everything."

He gripped Charles' hand firmly, gazing intently at the older man, their look communicating more fully the words of their final parting. "Godspeed, son," Charles whispered. "Go with God. Do not forget, your strength lies with Him. Godspeed."

As Peter passed back through the kitchen, he exchanged farewells with Shawna and Loressa who were engaged in the final supper preparations of the Taylors. He grabbed his rifle and slipped out the rear door of the cabin and started for the woods where he knew the runaways awaited him.

"Peter!"

He turned around sharply at Henry's voice. The boy had burst out of the back door of the cabin and was racing towards him. At a slower pace than Henry had adopted, Peter started towards his young friend. Reaching him, he knelt down before the boy on one knee. "What is it, Henry?"

"Peter," he cried, the tears beginning to pool in his eyes, "why do you have to go?"

Peter bit his lip, searching for how to explain it. "I know I said a lot of things before—"

"You said that war was not a game, that it was evil!"

Wincing as he recalled the memory, he continued, "I know I did, and I still believe it."

"Then why are you going? Why can't ya just stay here with us?"

He laid a hand gently on his shoulder. "Henry, I have to go. The army needs soldiers to help oppose those who are invading our land. This war is lasting longer than most people expected, and the Union is growing stronger. William and James have already answered the call, and I feel that I need to take my stand beside them." He looked deeply in the boy's blurry eyes. "Do you understand?"

Henry nodded slowly. "Yes, I think so."

Giving the boy's shoulder a final squeeze, Peter offered a small smile of encouragement. "I will be thinking about you each day."

"I'll be thinkin' 'bout you too. Here," he dug into his pocket, "take this. I made it." He handed Peter a small, wooden cross. Peter took it, twisting the object in his fingers as he examined it. The cross was rather rough, and though it was only a few inches high, Peter felt the threat of tears in his own eyes.

He looked up at Henry. "You made this?"

The boy nodded. "Yes. I want you to take it so you will know that Jesus is always with you, and that He loves each of us, just like you had said."

"Thank you, Henry." Peter slipped it into his own pocket. "I will always keep it with me."

He glanced back towards the cabin and found two figures standing in the rear doorframe. Squinting slightly, he realized the figures were Jenny and Emily, watching his departure. How he would miss his neighbors, but he had to go.

Turning his head back to gaze fully at the boy, Peter continued, "I...I have to go now. Good bye, Henry. Take care of yourself."

"Goodbye, Peter," Henry returned, the tears brimming again.

Rising, Peter turned and resumed his former path, not trusting his own emotions to remain under control if he waited any longer. As he reached the top of the first rise, he took a final look back towards the cabin. Henry was just reaching the door way and, realizing his friend had stopped, offered a final, vigorous wave. Peter returned the motion, then plunged on his way.

Reaching the door of the old shed, he rapped the quick three knocks and slipped in, letting his eyes adjust to the darkness. As the room came into focus, he surveyed the five Negro men and woman who stood before him. He tried to smile. "My name is Peter. I will be your guide. Before we start, I need to warn you—there are slave catchers in these parts. Silence is an imperative. The Taylors and myself have been praying, and are continuing to do so, and I give you my word that I will give my life to see you safely to the next station." He surveyed the faces that gazed back at him. "Alright, let's go."

They slipped out the back door he cracked open and began racing down the trail he indicated. The sinking sun cast deeper and deeper shadows which began to blend with the fading light to form a gathering darkness, threatening to envelope the countryside before much more time elapsed. Peter knew the way thoroughly, having traveled it many times before, but his eye was even more alert than usual that night. Perhaps it was the knowledge that the slave catchers were near at hand, or maybe it was the realization that it was his last run with the Underground, he didn't know. He didn't even know if he would make it safely to the next depot with all of those in his charge or if he would make it to the army to enlist. What he did know was that he had chosen to follow the Lord, and he would obey Him regardless of what the future held.

TIMELINE

1860

September—The beginning of *The Choice*

November—Peter discloses his past, visit from Olivia and Lawrence

December 20th—South Carolina secedes from the Union

1861

January 9th—Mississippi secedes

January 10th—Florida secedes

January 11th—Alabama secedes

January 18th—Peter joins the Underground

January 19th—Georgia secedes

January 26th—Louisiana secedes

February 1st—Texas secedes

April 12th—Fort Sumpter is fired upon, first shots of the war

April 17th—Virginia secedes

April 19th—Union blockade of Southern ports begun

May—Volunteers from Chesson plan to enlist

May 6th—Arkansas secedes

May 20th—North Carolina secedes

June 2nd—Farewell celebration for the Chesson volunteers

June 8th—Tennessee secedes, Confederacy completed

July—Union blockade completed, all major Southern ports guarded by Federal Navy

July 21st—Battle of First Manassas (Bull Run); first major land-battle of the war, Confederate victory

August 10th—Battle of Wilson's Creek (Oak Hills); first major engagement of the west, Confederate victory

September 12th-15th—Battle of Cheat Mountain; first engagement led by Robert E. Lee, Union victory

October 7th—Peter receives letter from his father

October 29th—Peter leaves to enlist

GLOSSARY

Accoutrements—Accessories, such as powder and percussion caps for a rifle.

Fugitive Slave Act—A law passed in 1850 that forbade any protection to runaway slaves and ordered the Federal government to assist slave catchers in returning runaways to their masters.

Hand Drill (Drill)—A tool operated by a crank handle that was used to bore holes into wood.

Hand Plane—A tool used for smoothing the edges and surfaces of wooden boards. Some planes had blades with specific profiles, enabling them to be used to carve designs along the edge of a board.

Knickers—Boys' pants whose length came between the knee and the ankle, worn usually till about the age of twelve.

Lathe—A machine powered by a foot-petal that rotates wooden cylinders upon an axis. The wooden cylinder was clamped between two rotating pins, and as it rotates, chisels were used to carve designs while decreasing the diameter of the cylinder to the desired measurements.

Missouri Compromise—A bill passed by congress that admitted Missouri as a slave state and Maine as a free state, and drew a dividing line between slave and free regions of the country in 1820. After this bill became law, any territory receiving statehood above the line was automatically a free state, and any one below the line was automatically a slave state.

Popular Sovereignty—The practice of giving new states being added to the Union the privilege of deciding for themselves whether they would be a free or slave state.

Station—The house or building that runaways hid in during the day as they waited to resume their flight at night.

Tongue (Wagon)—A wooden bar attached by a pivot point to the front axle of a wagon or farming implement. To this bar, the draft animals' harnesses were attached to permit them to draw the load behind them.

Underground Railroad—The secret network of individuals who either led runaway slaves between stations or provided protection in their homes, or both. It was an informal system, information concerning it being spread almost exclusively by word of mouth.

THE CHESSON VALLEY SERIES

In the years surrounding the brutal American Civil War, Peter Brenton finds himself faced with many decisions, decisions that will change his life forever. In the first book, *The Choice*, Peter is drawn into an underground network devoted to bringing freedom to slaves. However, he begins to feel the mounting pressure as his nation moves ever closer to the growing threat of war. In book two, *The Cry*, Peter and his comrades find the conflict to be lasting far longer than anyone imagined, and to be of incalculably greater cost. He wonders how his nation will ever be restored. In the final book, *The Change*, Peter returns to Chesson a defeated man, struggling not only with the recent loss of the war, but also with his own inner turmoil. The horrors that he had seen and experienced leave him questioning where the Lord has been, and as he attempts to resume his former life, he searches desperately for answers. What he finds shocks even him.

From the next book in the Chesson Valley Series—

As the cannons continued to fire relentlessly, Durran slipped into the entrenchment between Caleb and Peter. "You boys alright?" he yelled.

"Yes," Peter returned, "you?"

"I reckon so, if I can keep clear of one of those," he ducked as a ball screamed through the air in the tree tops. "They've been getting pretty close, too close!"

"That they have!" George yelled. "Someone needs to tell our artillery to answer!" Caleb emphatically called from his other side.

"No, not yet," Durran returned.

"Why the dickens not?" George incredulously retorted.

He pointed towards the smoke in the valley below. "If we open fire, them Yanks will know exactly where our cannons are! Right now, they're just shooting in the dark, just shooting away like blind men. I say, let 'em! We'll just stay low and stay ready."

Another ball screamed through the air, and once more they ducked in response. Raising his head, Peter inquired, "Have you heard what is happening up there?" he nodded towards the firing to their north.

Durran nodded. "Those hills up there, they call 'em Marye's Heights. Longstreet's got his batteries up there, and I heard the Yanks are trying to take the hill, but he's holding them back pretty good."

"I hope he can hold."

"Me too," Durran nodded grimly. "If either his line or ours breaks, those people yonder will sweep up behind and take the rest of the army. We've got to hold this line!" A cannon ball stabbed the earth, initiating the spray of dirt and grass.

Peter did not know how many had been killed so far by the bombardment to their line, but he had seen Stuart's artillery plow through the Union lines, and he knew that Longstreet's artillery had a brutal aim. On both sides, blood had been spilled already, and he knew the day of slaughter was only starting to commence.

Slowly, almost imperceptibly, the cannonade began to subside. One by one, the Union artillery ceased their firing. The only sounds that continued was the sporadic firing to their north and the ringing in their own ears, but for their immediate vicinity, an unnerving silence prevailed. It could only mean one thing, Peter knew.

The rattle of drums began to sound, faint. Faint, but still audible, it gave credence to Peter's assumption, a conviction mirrored in the set jaw and determination blazing in the eyes of his comrades. Hesitantly, Peter raised himself and peered over the breastwork into the smoke lined valley below…